NO ALABASTER BOX

NO ALABASTER BOX

*dedicated to
Olivia Brose
With best wishes
from the author
Charles D. Bradley*

Charles D. Bradley

10/16/05

Copyright © 2005 by Charles D. Bradley.

Library of Congress Number: 2004098655
ISBN : Hardcover 1-4134-7570-1
Softcover 1-4134-7569-8

All rights reserved. No part of this book may be reproduced or transmitted in any form or by any means, electronic or mechanical, including photocopying, recording, or by any information storage and retrieval system, without permission in writing from the copyright owner.

This is a work of fiction. Names, characters, places and incidents either are the product of the author's imagination or are used fictitiously, and any resemblance to any actual persons, living or dead, events, or locales is entirely coincidental.

This book was printed in the United States of America.

To order additional copies of this book, contact:
Xlibris Corporation
1-888-795-4274
www.Xlibris.com
Orders@Xlibris.com

27157

This book is dedicated to my wife,
the love of my life,

Mary Morey Bradley

ACKNOWLEDGMENTS

The Florida Keys by Joy Williams, Random House 1987
No Alabaster Box by Eve Lynn, Alpress 1936
The Sun Goddess by Sheena McGrath, Cassell 1997
A Dream of Countries Where No One Dare Die by Louis Phillips, Southern Methodist University Press, 1993

These works all were helpful and inspirational to me, and for that I thank the authors.

Also I thank:

Cheever Tyler, Natalie Melbardis, Tyler Reigeluth, Susan Reigeluth and Vicky Chave Clement
Good friends all.

It is the right time for looking back through time to yesteryear-take stock, look back, examine where I've been and what I've learned, old lessons re-examined, newer lessons perused slowly and in peace. I'm on two roads which have converged today with great clarity: one, the road through convalescence from a grave and serious illness, the second, the road of contentment: sitting on a sun-filled porch balcony on a perfect Maine summer day, the great firs sighing in the light breeze, a large hillside covered with ferns falling away to a distant blue sea foaming about large granite boulders. Eternity, and my place in it and my eventual rest in it, have loomed large lately. Anxious consultations with doctors, with my lying helpless amidst an octopus of tubes and drip bottles, the worried, even haggard face of my beloved Alicia, straining to catch the doctor's words. I was in danger of losing my humanity during this time. I became an entity, "the patient" (the irony of that word) to be poked, watered, fed, cleansed, colonically irrigated, in a world clinically sterile. Personality quickly vanished, as did modesty; even humor seemed to have little place in the scheme here. I was a package of goods and services to be examined plugged, unplugged, perhaps dispatched, who knew where?

And then this phase ended, rather abruptly as it turned out. The tubes and bottles were effortlessly and speedily removed, I was upended almost with a jolt and returned to the world of the living, silently wheeled to the waiting car and home.

The apartment I returned to was a small one bedroom in an old Pre-World War II building in the East 80's of New York City. Alicia and I use it as a pied-a terre when we feel the need for city living, spells that occur farther and farther apart now that our son Kip has grown, married and has a young family of his own in LA.

In getting out of the cab I nearly collapsed into the street but for the catching arms of Amos Jorkins, our doorman,

"I've got you, Mr. Rushing, easy now, Mr. Rushing no worry now. Good to see you coming home Mr. Rushing," as he effortlessly guided me through the lobby to the waiting elevator. "Don't try to overdo, now. Just take it easy" he clucked like a rotund hen scolding an errant chick. He pushed 8 and the doors closed.

For two weeks I lay in bed only crawling to the toilet. Alicia shaved me with an electric razor, a mode necessitated by my weakened condition, but one which I personally loathe. However, too weak to complain I bore it all. The doctors prescribed a convalescence at High Keene, Alicia's family country house on the Maine Coast, just as soon as I could stand the drive. This didn't occur for another three weeks.

Alicia, ever watchful of my moods and overall condition, determined June 20th as the day "you need only sit in the car. Amos and I can load. You've taken care of me as long as I can remember, now it's my turn."

Meekly assenting in all this, I sat in the back seat as the bags and baskets were loaded aboard, and we set out for the North Country.

A word or two about High Keene and Alicia come in here. The house is a simple Maine farmhouse originally built as an egg farm. Having any frontage on the sea was happenstance, but in my lifetime it was made more attractive as a country place. Alicia's father, Theron Salisbury, had inherited it from an old-maid cousin. She had taken him in during his teen years when both his parents had died in a flu epidemic within five days of one another. "Aunt Hen" had provided for the boy including helping to send him to Bowdoin College. The young Theron became a thinker early in life eventually starting an aircraft parts manufacturing company. He became what a local newspaper of the time termed "One of the Maine's Captains of Industry." In the bigger picture he was a minor "captain", but it was considerable by Maine standards of the time. His wife, whom I never knew, she having died early on, was a member of a minor sprig of the extended Vanderbilt clan. This provided the young Alicia (an only child) with distant cousins throughout the New York-Palm Beach-Santa Barbara social scene.

However, Alicia was afflicted with slight deafness

from birth. This led her to having a "difficult" reputation socially, making the frivolity of upper crust New York an impossibility for her. She was, I know now, lonely and miserable, but what it achieved was a firm attachment to her father of an intensity way beyond the norm. The two thought alike, shared every impulse, every company problem. They were mirrors of one another even to telepathic communication of vein similar to twins.

This introspective cast to Alicia's personality was the main reason for her eventual interest in me. Had she had normal communication with the world at large I know I would have been of but passing interest to her as the male nurse and companion of the ailing father, which I was. She had the stalwart silence almost of the Indian, the knowing eternal "seeing out at time and space" which I so valued in my own father's Indian streak. Since I took care of her soul mate in his time of need, she focused her sights on me as a total individual, studied me, weighed my pros and cons, with the intensity she had developed (so early in her own life) due to her perceived handicap. I became a necessary part of her universe of caring for and loving her god. Call this symbolic if you so wish, but it is the only explanation I can give as to why Alicia and I eventually became one. Nothing else fits such two polar-apart people as Alicia and I, the backgrounds, "the all of it" that is us.

* * *

My mother had always held a certain mystery to me, probably due to the element of mythology and legend surrounding her mother's family. My mother was of pure Lettish ancestry, Laima Saule Neikens Rushing was her full name, and she was of a line that was still revered in Latvia as the keepers of the pagan flame of the sun-worshipping pre-Christians. Latvia's agrarian culture still pays credence to the "old ways," when the moon is propitious for planting crops, when to harvest, what to harvest first, what oak trees should be planted where, all that storehouse of ancient lore slipping back thousands of years in Lettish folk tales. "Saule" means "sun" in Lettish, just as my second name "Meness" means "moon". The females in her mother's line all carried "Saule" just as the males, myself included, carried "Meness." The moon and the sun mated in Lettish lore. Then in a contemporary twist (so I felt anyway) the moon was unfaithful, and seduced "Auszrine" the Goddess of the Dawn. This bit of folklore later became interesting as explaining why my mom was not angry with my father when his extracurricular "career" came to light. After all, the gods had been unfaithful 6000 years ago—no big deal.

My mother had an "otherly" look to her, as young women appear in old fairy tales. She was rather short, small waist, larger hips, and puffy cheeks with a tiny mouth which pursed like a kitten's. Her father on the other hand was the classic peasant, abrupt, hard drinking, greedy, close mouthed, often brutal. He owned a tavern in Secaucus, New Jersey and kept pigs, which were nurtured by New York City's garbage. His barn was the source of smuggled alcohol, later untaxed cigarettes, I learned only later in my teen years, and porno movies.

My mother, once her mother died, became partially estranged from her father. She became a nurse working first in Newark Hospital and later at another in the Bronx. She was a nurse by instinct, careful, mindful of instructions left her by the doctors, thorough. Coming from a line of priests and priestesses made ministering come naturally to her. I never knew until my barn discovery, how she ever had met and married my father. But marry they did, and soon my father learned of a bar in New Rochelle which had living quarters above and two small rental offices. It was in foreclosure, and could be had cheap. My mom and dad moved out of the house in Secaucus to the Mercury Bar and Grille in downtown New Rochelle, leaving my grandfather to his various shady activities in the blacksnake-infested hummock in the marshlands of New Jersey. This was when my mom started nursing in the Bronx Hospital which was only a short way from New Rochelle.

My mother never talked about first meeting my father, or where it happened, or why. It was a closed subject, but shortly after we moved, my father seemed to spend less and less time at home. Often, he would be away for days, sometimes weeks. He would be away all night, walk in as I was leaving for school and sleep all day, getting up while I would be doing homework, sitting at the kitchen table. I learned to cook early as my mom worked medical hours and would take the local from 125th Street to New Rochelle and walk home from the train station, often arriving at home at 8 or 9. Sometimes my father would bring home wide-ranging collections of items. Once 500 pairs of nylon stockings appeared, I remembered another time thirty bottles of high-grade brandy. One morning he walked in lugging a television set and I remember how proud I was to have a TV long before my friends at school. Being an only child made me happy to be alone, and I rarely had friends over after school. I remember my parents never nagged me about bringing kids home; they seemed to be loners themselves, and the fewer people around, the better. Years later I knew why this was the case, but my childish innocence kept me unaware of anything unusual until I was practically grown.

Then I turned fourteen. My father had been away off and on more than usual, there had been some phone calls which he would not take, but would go downstairs to the Mercury to return. My mother looked worried more often than I had ever remembered. She had been having trouble at the hospital with an incompetent supervisor, and in my naivete, I merely put it down to that.

Then one February day, I arrived home from school to find the two of them sitting in the kitchen. I was stunned. I hardly ever saw them at the same time, much less my mom home like this. What had happened? Grandpa Neikens had died was all I could think. Not that he and my mom had gotten along well these past few years. I personally could take him or leave him, but "family is family" and blah, blah, blah.

So all this flew through my mind as I was standing there in the kitchen, faded cracked linoleum floor, high legged gas stove, the clean but old-fashioned room, with its high ceiling and string-pulled fluorescent doughnut of a light, the center of our family life.

My father was going away, my mother said.

"He's found work out West" in Binghamton, she said. She used "he" like a stranger, like my father wasn't even there. And my father didn't even speak while she said this. He stood rock-silent looking. I called it his Injun look, which took you in, but then seemed to go through you to stare at a far-distant lake or mountain or something like that. I know now that it was that his mind was working on two distinct planes-one the here and now, the other the look beyond the petty trials and tribulations to eternity. Like he could see "the all" way beyond the cares and woes of now.

Then he put both his hands on my shoulder and said,

"Be a man from now on," he then looked at Mom and said to me, but still looking at her, "Be good to your mother, help her all you can and remember the things I told you."

Then he turned to my mother and said almost casually, "I've got to see George for a minute. I'll meet you downstairs." (George McManus was our lawyer-tenant outback). Then he was gone. My mother picked up her cloth coat lying on the back of one of our green wooden kitchen chairs and followed him down the stairs. I had not spoken one word. I was still thunder struck. I walked over to the window that looked out onto the alley. Two signs hung from our building over it. They marked the two offices located in the space which was part of our building behind the Mercury. "George McManus Attorney-at-Law" said one, the other was "Estep Janitorial." That sign always seemed incomplete to me, Janitorial what? Services, functions, maybe. But it was good enough for Clem Estep, who was a hillbilly from West Virginia and wasn't too particular about the Queen's English.

 Through the bar window I could see the reflection of the "mercury" neon sign which hung out over the sidewalk on the street side of the building. It was a big blue neon sign of a foot with a wing attached to it, that being the sign for Mercury the God. I went through the motions of preparing dinner completely in the dark as to who might be eating it. My mom? My father? Neither? Both? Mom always told me what was what for the dinner hour, what time she'd be home, what train, or if her friend Elena Stimma, who worked at the same hospital and lived in nearby Port Chester might be giving Mom a lift.

 As I've said, my mom was a bit of a mystery to me. She had no facial expression (and with that no wrinkles either). Her skin was very white, pallid I think says it best, it never tanned in summer, she never blushed; it stayed white, the white you see on the underside of some mushrooms. It didn't appear human somehow, but more like that of a moon maiden. That's a long way of saying I could read nothing on her part of just what was going on in her mind. And my father saying. "Remember the things I told you." That sounded not only serious, but final. My father, when I had been alone with him, had told me a lot about Indian lore, how to walk without putting any weight on my feet, how to fry acorns and how to accept punishment without flinching. How to extract vengeance afterwards as well. Vengeance was a very strong part of what he termed "the Indian mode," and the trickery it could take sometimes frightened me.

I waved as I saw Jonas Soltis the Mercury barkeeper who had taken over running the bar for my father (my mother really) when my father was away so much. Jonas, too was a Lett, who had worked for my grandpa at the Riga Bar in Secaucus.

He leaned out of the Mercury window, as the frigid air turned the warm bar air almost to steam. "Your ma won' t be back for awhile. You can come on down here if you want," he said.

I nodded "no thanks" as we both closed our respective windows against the rapidly approaching darkness and cold.

I ate alone and went to bed around 9:30. I heard my mother come in, kick off her boots and shut their bedroom door. Then silence.

My father is probably the most complicated piece of the jigsaw puzzle that was my family. Most of the twists and turns of his personality I pieced together much later than these boyhood years I have been talking about. I most clearly understood him during long nights of sitting in aide stations in Chattahoochee or sitting with Theron Salisbury through long stretches of his sleeplessness.

Rod Rushing was a chameleon. His race was mixed. His own father Delmus Rushing was part-white, part-black and part-Indian, whether Seminole or Caloosa, I'm not sure. Delmus hailed from the panhandle of Florida, from what in Florida was termed "the western highlands". This area was right against the southern bound of Alabama, the hills were probably no more than 400 feet high, but that counts for a "highland" in Florida. He and his brother had both left home early and before long they realized they could "pass". And pass they did. Delmus eventually ran a roadhouse near New Orleans, sold bootleg, counterfeited money, ran arms to Central America aboard small boats and became involved in what was a family niche business for himself and his son Rodney, namely manufacturing and selling silencers for firearms, a highly illegal and highly paid vocation. One pinch from the long arm of the law landed Delmus in the jurisdiction of Florida, Orlando to be exact where he encountered Gayle McKinstrey, a Scotch-Irish hillbilly from the North Carolina Smokies. She was proprietor of a bail bond establishment, one of the first women in the country to be so, and my grandmother. Grandma Rushing carried a gun and was a bounty hunter without peer. Delmus learned this to his chagrin and discomfiture. His brother Grail Rushing (originally Holy Grail Rushing, then refined to H. Grail and finally, as part of the passing process to just Grail) came to Orlando to help Delmus jump bail and incidentally to deliver a shipment of silencers to Galveston. Unfortunately the ship in Galveston was impeded by a storm and the Rushing brothers were delayed for a week. They had moved into a "fancy house" in Galveston which had known them both, when tragedy struck. "Miz McKinstrey," as she was always known, strode up the steps of the Silver Slipper and caught both brothers in the arms of the beauteous Ramirez sisters. Grail, she had no hold over, but $5,000 of her money was riding on Delmus. He was hauled back to Orlando to face trial. The silencer shipment was delivered and Grail, richer by $30,000 hired the foremost defense attorney in northern Florida, Cloyce MacFadden Jones of Tallahassee. Jones, known as "The Cat" to the bar (legal not drinking) destroyed the States case and set Delmus free, but not free of "Miz McKinstrey" who married him soon thereafter.

Rodney was the lone offspring of this arrangement and definitively took his father's looks. Delmus had the string moustache look of a Spanish don and the slightly curly tight hair of the octoroon. The old sepia photo I remember having in New Rochelle is long lost, but the overall countenance was that of the matinee idol of the period.

By the time Rodney had matured, he had been involved in silencer-making to a degree that had brought him to the attention of the FBI. He had had, I later learned, a small manufactory in Cleveland which was fronted by an autobody shop run by one of Rodney's darker cousins. It was watched, then raided, by the FBI. Rod barely escaped. He drove east, ending up in New Jersey where luck would have it, he met Grandpa Neakins in Secaucus. A deal was struck, and part of Grandpa's barn suddenly emerged an autobody shop. The cars being "worked on" stayed a long, long time in the yard. Once when I was quite young maybe six-we hadn't moved to New Rochelle, I wandered into the barn, something I had been strictly forbidden to do and found a room there set up as a bedroom. Two or three hard backed chairs, a fringed bedspread over the bed, and one of the interior walls of the room cut away leaving an open space from about 3 feet off the floor up to the ceiling. A small room, little bigger than a closet, was next to the bedroom on the opposite side of the opening. There was a stanchion on the floor of this smaller room on which something could be placed which could capture what was going on in this bedroom.

Jonas, Grandpa's bar keep didn't live on the place. Who could be sleeping in this room, I wondered, as I fingered the fringe hanging floor-ward from the bed. I had never seen a soul in the way of anyone remotely living on grounds. But I had heard trucks at night coming to the barn. It was all very mysterious to a small child, and I knew two things: first, that I should not have been there and second, that I could never ask anyone in the family, including Jonas, what it all meant. Even at this early age I had learned not to question anything my parents or grandfather did, what they did or did not say or where they went. My father even then, was often away or closeted out in the barn. I learned to sweep out the tavern early in the morning before it opened up and tended a hencoop out back near the piggery. From the very first the barn was forbidden.

Though it was of formidable size and had numerous rooms and compartments inside including several doors which seemed to open from several of these compartments directly to the outside, it was never once mentioned in the conversation in the years we lived there. The tavern was a separate building on the other side of the house with the piggery behind that. The barn was slightly isolated from the living and working areas of the house and tavern.

The barn with its enticing mysteries faded a bit in my consciousness once we moved to New Rochelle except for the one incident which occurred during a short visit I made back to Grandpa's one summer.

Two neighboring boys, Sammy Toducci and Stan

Nelski had been acquaintances of mine in my early school years. Playmates-no. Even then, somehow playmates were discouraged, but as I have said, being an only child seemed to make me perfectly happy being alone and having myself as company. But on this particular visit I ran into Sammy and Stan. Stan was extremely mature for his years, we were maybe fifteen or sixteen when this happened, "Hey Gil (my name was Egils shortened to Gil) so we're hearing from the grapevine some hotsy stuff going on at night in your old gramp's barn. You heard anythin' about that? Hey Gil?"

Sammy jumped in with, "Yeah, real good stuff big New York (he pronounced it "Noo Yawk") cars coming up your back dirt road. We seen 'em."

Apparently they'd found a spot on the barn roof with an overhanging branch of a large catalpa tree where you could sit on a branch and look into an upper window.

"We'll go tonight," says Stan.

"How do you know we'll see anything," say I.

"Cuz we been watchin' this place past two three nights and cars been comin' in," this from Sammy.

It looked to as though they hadn't quite had the courage to actually go up the tree and see for themselves. They were using me to bolster their courage. But then for the first time it struck me: hey I was old enough to be a man and know things. Enough mystery for crissake, what the hell is goin' on in that barn?

"Ok" I say "meet me under the tree tonight at what

time? Eleven thirty ok? Is that when it goes on? And we'll do it."

They both nodded yes, and that night we met. I should say I had been left off at Secaucus alone to go to Grandpa's, my father being away as usual and my mother tied up with a private case in Westchester which was proving a windfall for us financially.

So it was a rare event me being there by myself with just Grandpa, Jonas having now gone up to New Rochelle to the Mercury.

By 11:00 that night I was looking out the attic window of the house which had a view of the barn. I knew Grandpa had disappeared out there around 9:00. The barn was pitch dark but there appeared to be several cars parked behind the barn where a dirt track snaked out from the barn to Route 3, the road into Manhattan.

The three of us climbed the tree and dropped on our bellies on the roof and shimmied our way up to the window. A curtain had been drawn across the window, but it had not closed tightly. We had a good view through the crack. A faint light flickered intermittently. My God, a movie!!

What was going on? A row of heads were visible on straight black chairs set up in the dark. They were watching a grainy "Heads or Tails" starring Christara Knight and Rod de Long. But what had me about to fall off my perch was the sexual equipment of Rod de Long—a salami came to mind and worse still I knew who Rod de Long was—my old man.

Neither Stan nor Sammy had ever seen enough of

my father to piece all this together, they were just in it for the action-and action there was plenty. Their preoccupation can only be described as glued. This gave me some time to digest all this.

A lot of things went through me like a kaleidoscope running on high speed. What could Mom think about all this? Did she know that Grandpa was involved in this? Was this why he and Mom were not so friendly anymore? Is this why we moved to New Rochelle? Was my mom angry with Rod (I couldn't call him Dad, that term seemed like a defilement suddenly). Was my mom (by moving to New Rochelle) trying to get Rod away from all this and away form Grandpa as well?

A tiny thought also crept in. The male hormones kicked in—holy cow I would never underestimate my own sexual equipment or prowess. Not now, no more. I was the son of Rod de Long and in every way shape and form.

I rolled away from Sammy and Stan, eased back down the barn roof and dropped down the tree into the barnyard. They never even knew I was gone. I had a lot to think about . . . a lot.

Another trait of mine, thoroughness, started during another trip away from New Rochelle. This one was on a visit my granma, "Miz McKenstry" Rushing in Lake City, Florida (she had moved there from Orlando after an altercation with a sheriff in Orlando had turned ugly). Delmus had left the picture by then and he and brother Grail had gone to California where they both were croupiers on a popular gambling ship. It lay just far enough offshore from Los Angeles to be in international waters.

My granma, as I called her was no-nonsense. If I was there, I was there to work, and no mistake. I read bail bonds at the Blue Bird Bail Bond Company which I learned had to be done carefully and thoroughly. Terms and conditions of bail could be tricky. One judge was prone to setting bail for culprits with set conditions. No more than thirty miles from court at any time until his court date (women were rarely arrested for bailable offenses in those days—they mostly shoplifted). Knowing where the culprit was at all times was particularly important to Granma. If she could catch someone thirty-two miles away she could increase her fees exorbitantly, since the culprit had broken bond and theoretically was in forfeiture. First time culprits were especially likely to find themselves in this fix. Habituals knew better and would stay put unless they broke bond entirely and fled the jurisdiction. We would spend a lot of time, Granma and I, doing what she'd call her "night work": driving around trying to find out if her victims were where they were supposed to be. This sort of work was congenial to my make-up, it fed on the sense of methodical thoroughness that I got from my mom. It also gave me two other "life rules," as I called them. First a respect for the letter of the law and have a healthy respect for lawyers, especially good ones, and second a burgeoning dislike of my father's character and his shady ways, sexual excitement notwithstanding. I hoped I had more character than he had, hoped I would not fall into his wonts.

Through long hot afternoons sitting in the Blue Bird office I heard almost all of what I now know of Rod. All except the Rod de Long part. I'm sure even now Granma never knew of this. On my return north to New Rochelle, I noticed another different and startling thing: my mom was more open with me, she must have felt that I was older now and that she could confide in me. My father was going away again, and this time there was no euphamism about "going west for work in Binghamton", it was hard time in the Big House. He had been caught red-handed "with the goods", the charges were Federal and no parole.

I think Rod had figured out the jig was up with me when he'd returned "from Binghamton" that first time and my attitude toward him had changed. The porno involvement was too much for me, especially in that I now felt a chivalric protection toward my mom. When he was packing up to leave, I was as distant as I had ever been to him. This upset mom a lot, and she started crying, something I had never seen her do. Tears came down, but pooled above her cheeks, which were too rotund to allow the moisture to head farther downward. She wiped her apron onto her eyes.

After he left, she said to me "he was not totally to blame in all the movie stuff. My father got him into it, said he was a colossal stud was how your granpa put it "That there was a treasure there that needed to get out," he said and the money was big. I was greedy too for the money, and I didn't mind spending it" she wiped that apron again across her eyes. This was kind of a final revelation for me because it showed me that she knew that I knew, although we'd never directly spoken of it, and I took it to mean that now all her cards were on the table and that there would be no more secrets between us. I felt I was head of the family now, and that I could shoulder responsibilities as a man.

Going back in time a short bit, just before Rod left for what I knew would be a long time I had gotten into some trouble with the law. It was minor kid stuff, but the judge had placed me on probation. George McManus, our tenant out back had gone to court with me. He had told the judge to structure a probation for me that included working as a go-for in George's office, similar to what is now called a paralegal. George had always liked my mom and me, and I think thought I might eventually become a lawyer. I also had a night job sweeping out offices around New Rochelle for Clem Estep, of "Estep Janitorial."

Both of these facts became vitally important in the grand scheme of things, both of these associations affected the course of my life in astonishing ways.

* * *

My mom seemed to get along fine without Rod as the next few years passed; I was very happily working for George during the day and working evenings for

Clem. Cleaning out offices was not an extremely taxing job, and I got to know my way around the lower Westchester environs extremely well. Mom was still nursing and seemed content. Only one time was a comment made that seemed on hindsight to explain her relationship to my father's porno making. She had had a blow-up on the phone with her father. Their relationship had been rocky throughout my growing up. He had always been hard drinking, and it had taken its toll, both on his body and his mind. He was short-tempered and abusive. He had become reclusive, had closed the tavern, and the police had to be called once by neighbors after he'd ordered two men he considered trespassers off his property with a gun. The gun had fired (I think accidentally; he was pretty muddled by this time from alcohol) and he was arrested. I saw the article in the New Jersey paper, which Jonas had gotten from a crony over there. The two trespassers were Sammy and Stan. Granpa was out on bail when he suddenly died. Mom and I went out to Secaucus to clean out the house and hopefully rent it out. That's when Mom said, "he was a thoroughly detestable character, he would have used his grandmother's bones to pry open a cash register." She continued packing up some old Polish china, "but I guess I was just as bad," as she turned away from and suddenly leaned into the storage barrel. Was she obliquely referring to Rod's "career"? I think so.

Mom was in Granpa's house (or it was now hers, as his sole heir) meeting a prospective tenant. I was packing the car for the trip back to New Rochelle when Sammy and Stan came by in Sammy's pickup.

"So, Gil there was sump'n real shady goin' on outside the barn about two months ago. There was a big fire burnin' outside the barn. Some sheets and bedspreads in flames and a lot of reels of film-boy those blew up real good—then the guy throws on a camera.

We're standing in the road watchin' and the guy catches sight of us-yeah and guess who? The guy with the huge dong from that flick we saw dat night" all this from Stan, with Sammy nodding like one of those bobblehead dolls you set in your car on the dash board, the one whose head bounces up and down. Then, Sammy chimes in: "and then next time we come by your old geezer is out shootin' his gun at us. Real zoo, huh?"

So Rod had gone out there once he knew he was going away "big time": and destroyed as much evidence as he could. It was just as well; I don't think my mom could have faced having to be confronted by all that stuff. Now I also knew what that stanchion in the little anteroom beside the bedroom was for-a movie camera- I could see the blackened shard of it among the cinders of the barnyard drive. It curved around the barn to the dirt track which had been used to enter the secret den off Rt. 3 from Manhattan by the thrill seekers looking for a horny evening of porno out in the marshes and pig farms of New Jersey.

I locked the barn and tavern up tight and walked into the house. Mom was just finishing up with the prospect, and I said, ostensibly to mom but really to the couple,

"Don't forget to tell them the barn and tavern aren't included." Then I turned and walked to the car.

George McManus was a born litigator. He was good on his feet in a trial situation and had a quick reply for just about everything. But, like many sole practitioners, the rent was paid from real estate transactions, the vernacular term was: "closings". As a paralegal (via apprenticeship, not education) I took care of the paperwork which a closing involved. Clear title was required of a seller in order to deed the property over to the buyer. This clearing of the title was an arcane niche occupied by an eccentric trade known as "title pickers" or more grandiosely "title searchers". They were reminiscent of the old journeymen typesetters of the olden era of country newspapers. "Livery of seizein, vest, remaindermen, estoppel by deed" these were the everyday shoptalk of the title picker. I got to know most of this curious breed of folk operating in Westchester County, New York. The bottom line of all this was that I fully understood at a very early age the in's and out's of the title conveyancing business. This became important as the corollary of what I've believed to be the pivotal event of my young life. The event which changed everything forever.

My father's involvement in highjacking, porno and the silencer business led him into the by-ways of the Mafia, which held northern New Jersey and lower

Westchester tight in its fist. I learned early to spot the signs of Mafia infiltration in North Jersey/New Rochelle life overall. One person I had seen hanging out in the Mercury was Sonny "Wolf" Lupo, a foot soldier, which is Mafia lingo for young punk down-in-the-ranks on the lowest rung of the hierarchy. Wolf was a drinker, gambler, car thief and burglar. He held some sort of position with the Royal Commercial Laundry in New Rochelle. It provided table linen and napery to the myriad Italian restaurants which were on just about every block of New Rochelle, Port Chester, Larchmont, Mamaroneck and into the Bronx. This was only a pro-forma position for Sonny (the company was owned by his uncle, also mob-connected) Wolf spent his days drinking and playing cards at the Pulchinella, a bar and grill two blocks east of the Mercury. He moved on in the evening to Jocko Adragna's, a roadhouse/ nightclub farther east still on the Boston Post Road. He often drove a two door Olds coupe, an extremely powerful "muscle car", and I often spotted it parked on the streets of these Westchester haunts he frequented. Otherwise he drove a black Lincoln Towncar, of which more later.

My mom and I grew closer still during this time. She now had no family left and rarely got mail from Rod. I think he knew that he had forfeited his parental rights over me. As far as I was concerned, this was certainly the case. The marital relationship with Rod seemed over as well. Divorce was not the automatic procedure then that it is now, but I think no one would have blamed my mom if she had sought one. I think

George might have brought it up, but who knows. Anyhow, she enjoyed her work. She owned the business and living quarters that was the Mercury building (a larger neon blue winged foot reopened on our roof as well). The house in Secaucus was rented on a long term lease to a couple named Rosevear, young newlyweds who both worked in two different manufacturing concerns in Hudson county. They wanted to be settled in one place fairly long-term while they saved up a nest egg for their own place.

The tavern and bar both remained empty. No one seemed interested in either one, the barn in particular had a sleazy reputation around Secaucus, and probably the tavern too. The pigs had long gone to a farm farther south. The whole piece of ground had a hangdog look, but it was a four acre parcel which might be valuable some day if Secaucus even began to grow. It had a frontage on one of the town's main thoroughfares plus access to Rt. 3 down the "get away" dirt track from the back of the barn.

Mom rarely drove the car. I used it for my legal work for George, errands mostly for the practice and also for my janitorial work in the early evenings for Clem. She would often walk to the Mercury from the train station which was not far from us.

One cold February morning I dropped her off at the station. I was due to pick up a notary in town and drive him out of town to Tarrytown to get an invalid seller's signature on a deed for a closing that afternoon. As she got out of the car, Mom turned and looked me straight on. "You know you're the only person except for my own mom, who you never knew, that I ever loved. The only one." It was as if she'd put quotes around "the only one." I kissed her cheek "I know Ma" I said as I drove off. There was a funny finality to it all that stuck with me throughout the day. A vague unease, not quite foreboding but kind of out-of-sorts. I had to work the janitorial shift a bit later that particular evening. It got dark early and started to rain, not snow or sleet, but one of those cold winter rains.

It was about seven when I pulled into our alley that ran along George's and Clem's offices down to the back. I locked the car and was walking back up the alleyway to our outdoor stairs which led upward to our living space over The Mercury.

Suddenly I hear a shriek of brakes, a kind of thump and a crash—metal splintering and chrome dropping heavily. A crowd had already gathered—The Mercury was full that night and as luck had it two police cars parked right there with two cops standing talking when the whole thing happened. They were already getting a blanket out from one of the cop cars to put over the body. I knew in an instant who had been hit. Mom had been walking up from the station in the dark and the rain when she was struck. There was a big dent in the hood of the Olds and the windshield was cracked. She had been hit hard, and Sonny the Wolf was already being handcuffed.

The ambulance was there in a flash it seemed, and I rode with them to the hospital. She never spoke during the ride, but moaned a few times. The medical attendant was working hard over her, and I couldn't see much in the dark. They took her to Greenwich just over the Connecticut line to the hospital there. But I knew it was hopeless. The attendant gave me a slight touch on my arm as I dropped down from the ambulance to the ground. "Too bad" he said "you got a tough break" was all he said.

I called George from the hospital payphone. I told him what had happened, and that Sonny the Wolf had done it.

"Oh my God." he said "that poor game lady. So much sadness in her life, and now this." "You won't believe this, but after you left from the closing today, I was recording the deeds in Town Hall and Gladys over there and I were just talking about Sonny."

"Sonny?" say I in the stupor of shock and grief "you mean Sonny?"

"Yeah, I tell you more when I get there. Sit tight."

The morning New York papers all carried the story, not because my mom was high up in the fame department but because Sonny's arrest was big news.

New Rochelle, NY (AP)—Salvatore "Sonny the Wolf" Lupo, 34 was arrested last night for homicide with a motor vehicle after striking and killing Laima N. Rushing, 40 of New Rochelle. Mrs. Rushing was a nurse employed at Bronx General Hospital in the Bronx Borough of New York City. Details on survivors were not available at press-time, but it is known that her husband Rodney Rushing is currently incarcerated in Federal Penitentiary serving a 20 year sentence for manufacturing and selling gun silencers. Mr. Lupo has a long criminal record including larceny, burglary, auto theft and numerous gaming charges. He is reputedly associated with the Carrado crime family. Alcohol testing results are not yet available, but police reported a strong odor of alcohol emanated from the car.

By the next day George was steaming. He had always been protective of my mom, but now he was steamed. His Irish was up big. This was when his story regarding Sonny began to get interesting. As he related to me, he'd been chatting with the town clerk as he was "bringing down the title." This occurs on the day the property was closed and was a check on the title from the date the title was searched until the date it was closed and the closing papers were recorded. George's friend, Gladys Lenway, usually watched the day book for George on the days she knew he was closing a transaction to be sure nothing new was recorded against the title to cloud the sale and prevent title from passing until this latest encumbrance was cleared (i.e. by paying the lien holder amount claimed from the seller's sale proceeds).

As George was checking the title on the bring down, Gladys silently pointed to a newly recorded Certificate of Descent to a Salvatore Lupo. The property in question was the commercial laundry site and came to Salvatore Lupo from his Aunt Concetta Lupo who had recently died. Mafia members never hold title to anything if they can help it. It leaves openings exposed for not only people who might want to sue them and lien their property but flags the property to federal seizure as a racketeering site.

McManus looked puzzled "these wise guys never do this. They never take title to anything. We all know that" he raised his eyebrow toward Gladys. "I see it came in from Tony Cortesi's office. He'd have Lupo immediately deed the property over to a strawman, or his girlfriend or a corporation. Anything to hide it, he added. "That's valuable property right on the Post Road like that. That's a huge risk they're taking and not like Tony at all."

Gladys winked "Last Tuesday, I mean day-for-yesdy Tony was in here on somethin' else and just happened to mention he's away today and tomorrow Thursday" she said. "A new paralegal, a young blonde she was, I never saw before today, came in and recorded it, These new young squirts never know what they're doing. Bet it came in the mail to Tony's office. Blondie opens it up and decides she knows it all—Tony's away so she waltzes over here and records it. Bet her ass-is-grass when he finds out, oom-boy" Gladys laughs, her earthy cigarette-stained voice coming out of her chest in a long chortle . . .

"Guess you're right, Glad, that's probable just how it did happen. You know everything, ole' gal. Boy, I wanna keep you on my side, that's for sure."

George and I were sitting upstairs in out kitchen when he told me all this "So, what you think I should do now that we know Sonny owns a building? A suit'll take time and once Tony Cortesi learns of the slip-up about recording something that shouldn't been recorded till they could hide title, he'll fix that double quick" said I.

"Yeah, I know that, but there's one chance. It is a long shot, but it might work. I did this once before years ago in a similar bad-news situation, and it stopped a closing till my client got some money from the sale."

"Go one, I'm listening" I sat up straighter in the kitchen chair.

"Well, it's called an 'equitable lien' it's not supposed to have any force at law but it can cloud a title enough so the searcher will bring it up in the preliminary title report or on the bring down depending on when it's recorded. A searcher will never just pass on it and not bring it to the seller's attorney's attention. Also the buyer's attorney won't give over the money to the seller once they know about it. You know I always have the title searched whether I'm on the selling side or the buying side. It keeps both sides from missing something important. I like to know what I'm dealing with.

Plus I just had a thought that's even one better—Judge Ostly owes me big. If I can get him to sign the lien, kind of approve it like, it would give the document a little more oomph—more force-like, more like it's a lien with a judgment behind it even though it's not."

The next morning I buried my mom—just me and George. I notified Rod but heard nothing back from him. George was cooking up the lien after the burial service and went to see Judge Ostly. The judge had read the papers and was sympathetic, though he warned George "for the record," that the document wouldn't hold water if challenged. It stated that the Estate of Laima Neikens Rushing represented by George McManus claimed $50,000 in damages for her wrongful death at the hand of Slavatore Lupo. It was signed by George, and written next to his name toward the bottom of the single sheet it said Approve: Ostly, J. It probable wasn't worth much, but it made George feel better, or at least less angry. But I didn't know then what was to happen the next day. Gladys recorded the thing at 4:00 just as the town office was closing.

Have you ever done something you know to be the "right thing to do," but then have that act open up something spectacular and completely unforeseen? You did the thing all right, but so much more—all good came of it?

I felt that way after my evening janitorial route that night. Pete Sunner also worked at Clem Estep. He was a sadsack-type guy, but I felt sorry for him. Anyhow, I was kind of looking forward to doing anything that night that would take my mind off my Mother's burial that morning. Plus a few days prior, Pete had told me he had big plans for that night with his out-of-state girlfriend who as visiting in New Rochelle and could I cover for him? I told him I would and he had given me his set of the various office keys for the places he cleaned out on his nightly run and a list of the places to go to cover for him. A good long evening to complete two circuits, his and mine, and to keep my mind off my troubles. I could not believe my eyes, when I saw that list. Number four was attorney Anthony Cortesi's office, I had the key . . .

I raced through the first three stops and there I was at Tony Cortesi's office. It looked like he had been away just as he'd told Gladys. Mail was piled neatly on his desk by that "Miss Fixit" paralegal. There was little to do there trash-wise since Cortesi hadn't been there, but two things almost jumped out at me. There was a full real estate closing file spread on the conference table all set for tomorrow. I say tomorrow because his calendar book was also opened to tomorrow and there for 10am it read: Lupo conveyance, under this it read 1) record Lupo Certificate of Descent. 2) Warranty deed out from Lupo to Galloways (whom I figured were the buyers). That certificate was not supposed to have been recorded. The para should never have recorded two days ago. It left the property wide open for me and my "equitable lien."

I had heard via George's grapevine one other fact. Normally Lupo's Mafia pals would have sprung for bail for him, especially if my mom's death had been a Mafia hit. It had turned out the alcohol level in his blood was miles above the legal limit. The mob was none too happy about one of its own running around drunk driving and killing people that weren't supposed to get killed and doing it in front of two cop cars and getting caught. There was trouble raising bail. Sonny had been let out this just past afternoon, due to some machinations of a crooked judge friend of the Lupo's, but because it was homicide, another $150,000 bail was due by 5pm tomorrow, or Sonny went back to jail. Sonny and his lawyer must be looking at this closing for $200,000 as pure-and-simple "there is a God", manna, manna, manna, and I do mean money from heaven. It meant it had to close at 10am for Sonny to stay sprung.

I could not wait to get through the schedule that night. I had done right by Pete, actually gone in to work on my mom's burial day and look what I found out!

George's mouth literally almost dropped out of his face when I stopped by his apartment on my way home. "This kind of timing never happens," he kept saying over and over. "I don't believe it."

"But it's true" says I "I saw it all right there in his book."

We drank a few beers but then George said "Not too much party tonight I've got a closing to attend to, and you're gonna come."

* * *

George and I were sitting in his office at five to ten the next morning when the phone rang. Sure enough, who but Tony Cortesi.

"Hey, George how ya doin'. We got a problem here wit' dis 'ting you put on da land records against Sonny. Da buyers won't close a closin' we got goin' here. Wad is dis here leen any way?"

"I'll be there in five," says George and hung up.

We whip out into George's car and head over to Cortesi's office.

George plants me in a little ante-room at Tony's office where I can hear Sonny screaming through the closed door. The blonde paralegal is nowhere in sight, and I was sure she had fled the jurisdiction by now. George goes in to the conference room leaving me to hear plenty through the transom.

"So what's dis?" I hear Cortesi trying to get a word in through Sonny's "what da' muttherfuck dis" and "muttherfuck dat". Cortesi was trying hard not to say too much to George to hear in front of Sonny, so Sonny wouldn't find out Tony's office had screwed up by recording Sonny's name on the land records too early. Then I heard Tony trying to reach Judge Ostly on the phone only to be told he was at a court hearing out-of-state and not available until way after five. Plus, Tony didn't know that we knew how hard-up Sonny was and how they desperately needed to hand $150,000 over to Sonny's bail bondsman by five under the terms of his judge friend's release order.

Lupo and Cortesi had no bargaining chips—George had them all. And Cortesi knew it and needed to get George out of there before he spilled any beans about Tony's dereliction loose in his office while he was away.

By eleven o'clock I decided I'd better not be found there, so I slipped away, back to George's car. At eleven fifteen George appears grinning ear to ear. "We got the bastard's. $50,000, the whole cahuna." By eleven twenty George had come out of the bank with the check certified. "That'll stop Tony from trying to stop payment."

Then I cashed the $50,000 at my bank, get a $40,000 cashiers check payable to me and $10,000 to George. Hell, he'd earned it.

George looked at me with a kind of funny expression, like now that the fun was over something was bothering him.

"It's time for you to lie low, kid, and I mean that no foolin'. You've crossed Sonny the Wolf, and he's out on bail for sure now and you've got a lot of his money. Sonny is no joke."

By 12:00 I was putting a few clothes in my old book bag from school. I stopped down at George's office. He was suddenly very stern-looking, like real serious business was at hand.

There were two deeds set out on his conference table, and they were awaiting my signature. "These two deeds, one for the Mercury building and one to the Secaucus parcel. I've run the title to me as trustee. Wherever you are—and I don't want to know, ya' hear—call me at 10am the first of each month so I can update you on anything's happening here."

This was the real world, real serious and real scary. I knew it and he knew I knew it. My life was on the line. I had a wad of dough from a Mafia hitman and he was gonna try and find me—like big time.

"And I need to give you this" adds George, almost casual-like. It's an envelope, sealed with my name written on it. I recognized my father's handwriting.

"Don't waste time opening it here. Do it once you're on the road. He left it for you back that first time he went away." He had stopped calling Rod by his name. It was "he" and "him". "Said if things got hot for you to give it to you. Figure that's now."

Then it was a sudden goodbye—there was really nothing more to cover—and for the first time George hugged me as we said goodbye—I guess he felt I was kind of his son after all.

I wasted no time getting out of New Rochelle. Already I was a fugitive looking over my shoulder. George told me much later not that not five minutes after I'd gone, a black car was parked across the street from where our alley came out on the street.

I gassed Mom's car up in Rye. And pulled over to try to catch my breath. This had been a day of days. Every event was huge in its importance, like you've had a lifetime of little small, sane days, kind of boring even, little sameness things, like the expression "same ol'", "same ol'", and then there's one day where every fifteen minute segment smacks of the momentous and you're going in slow motion trying to keep up with it all.

My entire life had totally changed between five minutes to ten—I looked at my watch—2:30.

I opened the envelope, a single sheet was all, like he'd handwritten it in a hurry on anything that came to hand. "Secaucus house, spare room, closet floor, loose board.

BE CAREFUL OF BOX more in book. Remember all I told you. Love Dad." That was all.

I glanced at my watch 2:40. The Rosevears would be home by 5:20-5:30. I needed to get to that loose floorboard pronto and being now a fugitive, they couldn't catch me there.

I started the engine and took off for Secaucus.

* * *

It was 3:30 as I pulled into the driveway. The house looked neat and tidy notwithstanding the winter cold with its gaunt trees and a forlorn flowerbed by the drive that had never been there before. I still had mom's keyring (I had left my keys to the Mercury and this house with George). I pulled the car far up the driveway and parked it behind the barn. That way, nothing could be seen of my presence from the main road. (I was moving amazingly fast going into "think like a fugitive" mode). The Rosevears were still at work.

I opened the back door and flew upstairs to what we'd always called the spare room, a normal family I guess would've said "guest" bedroom—since we never had guests, I can see now why it would never have been called that. As a matter of fact, I don't recall the word "guest" ever once being used in any context whatever in our crazy family.

The Rosevears did have it as a guestroom, with cheerful curtains and a white bedspread with red poppies sewn on it. The closet was empty of clothes. Sure enough, after I had worked on the floorboards a bit, two popped up, exposing a cache hole beneath.

First I pulled up a little book, it was a book of poetry from the thirties with a soft red binding, *No Alabaster Box* the cover read, by Eve Lynn. Under the book in the cache hole was a solid metal, small box, say 6x8 or 9, a jewelry box. The edges around the opening were encased in a kind of sealing wax substance which would need to be melted off for anyone to open the box. The box was unlike anything I had ever seen before, no markings or designs, rounded corners, which would make it slippery to hold onto while opening it. Made of this shiny metal. A faint glimmer crossed my mind. Rod's checkered career had included a stint in the merchant marine and during the Second World War he'd been on a run to Greenland to get a shipment of some new metal called cryolite. I'd had a little walrus made of this substance as a child which he'd given me, and the metal sort of reminded me of that. I glanced inside the poetry book: "To mom from Delmus—Merry Christmas." Probably got to Rod in going through his father's stuff, Grail and Delmus being both dead and Delmus having retrieved it from his mother's things from her tiny house in Peaceton, Florida.

 Time it was a-flitting, I needed to get out of there, and fast. I stomped down the floorboards and carried the two items out to the car. I could ponder over all this later. Now I needed to put mileage between me and Sonny. I could just make out the remnants of the dirst track out the back of the barn. I took it, thinking as I did—"probable the last time in a long time I'll do this—maybe forever," as the car bounced along thought the marshes.

I drove till exhaustion set in. I was fueled on adrenaline from all the events of the day and the running. I pulled into a motel in northern Virginia and collapsed into the blackest, soundest sleep of my young life.

* * *

My father loomed large the next few days in my thinking. Firstly, because of these two items of mystery I carried tucked into my knapsack. And his letter (note really) to me and the fact that so much of my daily life and thought processes involved my mom.

My dad's influence had waned—he was no longer part of my life—I never felt disgraced by all he'd done, somehow, maybe due to my Lettish Grandfather's peasant avarice and greed having gotten into me. My mom never seemed to feel disgrace either, maybe she thought disgrace was for rich people, the poor just needed to get on, and get on she did in her tough, methodical, thorough nursery way, ever tending some priestly flame she no longer knew the old meaning of, but tend she must.

But now Rod was back in the foreground of my life. My mom was dead and buried, in the little Polish cemetery in New Rochelle; we could never find one for the Lettish dead. My dad was trying to tell me something I would need to know to survive. "My dad?" It was peculiar, but here I was saying it. It had been "Rod" to me in my own thoughts or "my father: if I referred to him to someone else. This latter rarely occurred since I didn't speak of him much.

But now I needed to study all this information he was handing me. I knew one thing though, for sure, my father's way of thinking, how he thought and what he believed, was what this all this meant. By the second night on the road at a motel in South Carolina I started focusing hard on Dad, his thoughts and especially how his mind worked.

I had not thought of that day when Dad left home for that fictive "work in Binghamton". But it came back like a scene in a move. He'd needed to see George for a minute. He was under pressure to leave. Therefore each word in that note needed to be analyzed word-by-word. He had left me spoken instruction which blazed across my consciousness, "be good to your mother, help her all you can, remember the things I've told you and be a man." I had been the dutiful and loyal son to my mom, and I had helped her all I could, and I think I had been a man. Now was the time for "remember the things I told you." This I went at with a will.

The South seemed to me to be a good place to reflect in. The weather was pleasant, which means you can wear comfortable clothes. You don't sit out of an evening reflecting if you have to spend ten minutes putting on heavy clothes to do it in. On a winter night in the North you can sit by a fire to reflect, but you have to tend to the fire, lug in more wood, keep it from sparking on lace doilies on your favorite chair. No place anyhow as a thought-provoking setting. There was a fireplace in

Secaucus, but I only recall one fire in it as a child. My mom was probably following one of her ancestral pagan urges and lit one. This infuriated her father for some reason. Maybe he thought she was wasting the furnace opening the flue. Anyhow, it was the beginning of my sensing that Mom and Grandpa did not see eye to eye about a lot of things. But I diverge. Back to the proper setting for reflection. I had spent very little time in the South growing up, but I had spent quite a bit of time with "Miz McKinstrey." As I've mentioned she was of mountain stock, Scotch-Irish, and was termed a "hillbilly or redneck" in the North, but termed country folk in the South. She wasn't p.w.t (pore white trash). She ran a thriving business and was exceedingly good at it, witness her capturing my grandfather Delmus Rushing. But she could tell a story, and these took us through many a slow afternoon. Tales of moonshiners and "revenooers", runaway slaves, and cruel overseers, second sight (which she claimed to have). This was Miz McKinstrey waxing heavy on a lazy afternoon.

The South has a tradition of reflecting—storytelling is the personification of it. There is still feudalism in the South. Tales of the lords and ladies carry over easily to the house on the hill and the doings of the fancy folk living in it. Add Indian lore which came easy to my dad and a dose of primal black lore which, whether he wanted to admit to it or not, was part of his psychic make-up.

So, southern Gothic tale-telling aside, I stared at my Dad's note "Secaucus house, spare room, closet floor, loose board" that part had all rung true to the letter. So far, so good. Next was "BE CAREFUL OF BOX." This was fast printed in block capitals like he'd done it in a hurry, but wanted to highlight it so I couldn't miss it. The box was more than locked; it was sealed. I was not to open it come hell or high water. Rod was reticent to a fault. He was as taciturn as the proverbial cigar store Indian. When he did speak, it meant something. It meant he had something to say and that something (and I learned to separate this early on in my thinking of and about him) that he was telling you was of importance and needed to be listened to and remembered. I cannot stress the importance of these spoken words. They came from the primal core of this man's very soul. It meant: this is how you need to live life. This fact is something I have learned and, by my speaking it, by my using the spoken word, means that I am making a great gift of this vitally important truth, encased in words spoken to you.

I'd picked up a Bible storybook somewhere as a child. In it was a picture of Moses, looking august and powerful with the tablets of the Commandments. My Moses was Rod and his rarely spoken words.

I need to add here that reticence was a big part of my mother's make up as well. She responded to my father's silences with ease, after all, keeping secrets had been part of my mother's family for thousands of years. She would receive Rod's pronouncements in silence, but I felt she agreed with them and "pondered them in her heart" as the Bible says. These two were amazingly well-matched; their silences spoke volumes in any other family. And of course I grew up thinking this reticence was fine and perfectly normal.

Two expressions stick in my mind about my dad's philosophy. He never said them but they were him. I think they were either bumper stickers or on those silly wooden plaques you see at summer beach or mountain resorts. One is "Don't get mad, get even" and the other is "revenge is a dish which people of taste serve cold". They both express the same theme, retribution, yes, but revenge. I say that also in two words: "Re Venge". Venge is awful, or as the kids today say it so lightly, "awesome." Awful—awe inspiring, because it's so horrendous, beyond description. Horrible. Nauseous to the onlookers sight of seeing it, it meant to my dad. "Vengeance is mine saith the Lord". No, vengeance is mine, saith Rod Rushing. His own corollary to this concerned forgiveness "I do not know what forgiveness means."

So what did the box mean? The way it was sealed meant it was not to be opened easily. You either had to melt the sealant off or somehow scrape it off, say with a knife. What might happen if someone did that and got it open. My first theory was of course some kind of bomb. You would open the box and be dead—A-ha, but if you're dead, where's the vengeance? You're gone, dead, it ain't there—so bomb is too easy. It's not that. Be careful of box. Care-be full of care. I didn't have a bomb in my hands, and it wasn't going to blow up on me. But take care of the box. Keep it safe, way from where it might be damaged or destroyed. Suddenly, the words "away from prying eyes" shot through me like a revelation. Was it an old fairy tale, is that where it came from? I didn't know, but that word "pry" seemed eerily à propos. And it fit with another saying of his "Keep yourself to yourself." Schoolyard bragging had always seemed foolish, and I was considered a loner early on. I was never bullied in school however, or taunted because another dad-ism was "Silence is power." No one can fight with you if you refuse to "play". Care to me meant "safe", kept safe from harm and kept to myself. No one should know I have this (not even George), and I should keep it safe from prying eyes.

The more I thought about all this I believed I had been given an instrument, one that was exceedingly dangerous to whomever it was wreaked upon. Wreak was it: wreak vengeance. Something so ghastly (an Alicia word!) that true vengeance would result. The mythological story of the man served a feast which he dispatched with great hunger and gusto only to be told his delicious treat consisted of his children roasted up for his delection. Now that's vengeance, the on-looker needs to find it as disgusting as the victim does.

Ok, so to the book. The book was not long, just a group of poems—so where to read the book. It suddenly entered my mind. Where was I going? Where was I to hide from this crazed goon who was out to kill me, without question. I'd been on the road two days and not a hint of where I was heading. I was in the South obviously, but why? And where to?

Ole' Dad suddenly hit me again "If you ever need

to disappear, the Panhandle will do the job" he'd said once. It had been said when we'd just received word that Delmus had died. Dad and his truck had gone off to California to tend to that. I'll bet that's where he picked up this little red book.

I cradled the book, stared at it. What could it tell me. Who was "Mom", my great-grandmother? The passing of Delmus and Grail into white mainstream commerce and society was one of Miz McKinstrey's stories, but I didn't know who was lighter, she? Her husband? For two children to have passed from Negro to white meant maybe both she and my great-grandfather were close on white. Were there darker siblings left behind?

I had an inkling yes, but not much to go on.

Where in the Panhandle had he meant? The only town ever mentioned, very vaguely, very shadowy, was Peaceton and Western Highlands. But looking at the book had lead me that far. At least now I had a destination—and it was one that I hadn't had till then.

"Always hide in plain sight," ok—so I'd go to Peaceton and then what? Here I was with what, to me, was a lot of money in my knapsack, a little red book, some changes of clothes and a way-too shiny box and what in hell was I supposed to do in Peaceton, Panhandle? So what was I to do in Peaceton to hide in plain sight and not stand out like a sore thumb, standing in the street directing traffic with my weird box shining like a beacon to oncoming traffic. Was there oncoming traffic in Peaceton? The next thought was another of those revelations. To hide in plain sight, do what anyone else does in Peaceton. That I'd need to find out when I got there. So get there I would and go from there.

The next day saw me crossing into Florida and turning west on Rt. 90, the main street of the Florida Panhandle. I went though Live Oak and Tallahassee. In Quincy, I rented a post office box. Farther west in Marianna I found a bank, opened an account, deposited the check and had the statements sent to my box. I wanted all this to be a bit away from Peaceton, so no one there would know I had any money. As I drove along 90, I noticed one thing that stuck me. The Panhandle was the dumping ground of the Florida penal system, there were work farms everywhere and barbed wire-encased penitentiaries and, as the crown jewel of all this, I drove by the Florida State Hospital, the insane asylum, right there on 90 in Chattahoochee.

"The reason God came to Florida is not because he needs a vacation, but because he wants to be close to Chattahoochee" was the standing joke in Florida. The Western Highlands were not for those who long for the mountains of either Scottish or the Rocky types of jagged terrain. The overall ambiance was retro redneck at its best. A perfect hideout, Dad was right. I practically fell into what became my first house within twenty minutes of my arrival. I had cruised Peaceton which took about three minutes. Heading back south towards DeFuniak Springs. I was held up by a construction crew that had set up shop since I had passed that way going into Peaceton. First I crept past one of those self-storage outfits where you rent a cubbyhole with an overhead on it. Then, across from that, Pinkston Termite Exterminators, and the Studdart Septic Service began to hove into view. Then I noticed a tiny house between the two behind a tangle of thicket of what looked like gigantic Jimson weeds. On the road was a forlorn looking mailbox with the faintest tracing on it: Rushing. I could just make it out. The driveway was nonexistent, but I saw where it had been and gunned the car through the high weeds and into the yard. It was a two-room shanty with a lean-to in the back. The main room had two old stuffed easychairs in it, a low table, and old kerosene lamp. Behind it was a narrow galley with the sink, old stove, newer refrigerator. The bath was rough, but usable and was off the kitchen. The back bedroom had an iron bed and a pile of blankets at the foot. Altogether a share-cropper cabin as seen throughout the country South. What clinched what I was suspecting was nailed over the bed: an old lithograph of a medieval knight in battle armor looking beatifically upwards at the chalice floating in the air above his adoring gaze (and surrounded by an intricate halo of light): it said in Gothic lettering below the picture "The Quest of the San Graal" and below that in parenthesis (Holy Grail).

My suspicions were right. I had stumbled upon what must have been Delmus and Grail's mama's cabin. From the road the lush undergrowth made the place totally invisible and the neighboring places were all commercial in nature. The highway signs for the termite and septic business carried your eye right past the place. The traffic moved swiftly past, this stretch of highway being a straightaway. I could get the mailbox down in a minute, Lord knows I sure wasn't going to get any mail! My knapsack and I were in that house in two minutes. I would need to replace the rusted lock and hasp which had allowed me to enter, but that was it. I pulled the car back behind the cabin and discovered something else that might prove useful: at the back of what passed for the rear yard, the faintest remains of two ruts passed through a jungle of Jimson weed. The track led to the back lot behind the septic place. That lot accessed not only the main road by going down either side of the little office building but also ran to a little used side road which led off the main road as well a little further down. An escape route if needed. Perfect. "Always hide in plain sight."

The next item of my plan was to get a job, blend into the local woodwork. I also didn't want to be seen around the cabin during the day. I figured the septic and termite people would be around during business hours. I needed to be gone by the time they arrived to open up for business and also gone around quitting time when they'd drop trucks off for the night.

"Hide in plain sight" began to nudge me toward the Panhandler's major mode of employment—guarding convicts. What better place? The next day I found myself, a member of the Florida Penal Service, working at a penal facility not twenty miles away. It was surprisingly easy—they needed extra personnel right about then due to a heavy influx of drug offenders needing to be housed and guarded.

That first night after work I started in examining the little red book of poetry. The inscription written in it had led me here to Peaceton, but I felt, I knew, there had to be clues from Dad in the book concerning the box.

The acre around the cabin was pit-dark—across the road was the self storage facility, three rows of short stubby, storage bins, each with its own metal folding overhead door, a bit menacing, glowering dully in the pale light of the lone street light along the stretch of road. The office there was pitch dark as were my adjoining office neighbors on either side, each with its own little fleet of trucks parked in their yards.

I had bought kerosene for my lamp and lying on the metal bed I began reading.

"Remember all I told you," he had been insistent on repeating that last line. "All I told you," meant I needed to try to remember every conversation I'd ever had with him. Volubility certainly wasn't part of him so this was by no means that difficult a chore.

A large segment of the Indian lore he gave me included a good deal about poisons. Indians used poisons on the tips of their arrows and on the blades of their knives. One story chilled me when he related it. He cast it in the garb of a "friend he knew" in the telling of it, and I wondered later if he himself had been "the friend" in question. Anyhow, the friend was an Indian who had been rudely insulted by the president of the local bank in the town. The banker was arrogant, obnoxious, patronizing—he ran the full gamut of inexcusable behavior. The Indian stood his ground, took the abuse, and never lost his composure or dignity. He was a meter reader for the local utility, and the next month, he had switched meter-reading routes with a colleague. Guess whose house meter was on his route. He went into the president's bathroom and smeared his razor blades with a poisonous substance. The prez nicked himself shaving and he was "toes up", as Dad described it, by two days later. There was a big funeral which the Indian attended.

A similar tale involved an Indian who sought and got vengeance in another way. He got a hold of his enemy's shoes for an incredibly short period. I think he was at the cobbler's and saw his enemy's shoes on the counter waiting to be picked up. While the cobbler's back was turned he inserted two tacks filed razor sharp into the toe of each shoe. You know the rest: the poison only took hours that time. I could see the victim hopping around after the tacks punctured his toes. Another adage of Dad's came to mind in connection with this story "how did the Indian wedge the tacks in so perfectly?" he smiled approvingly because I had asked the right question, "Always ask the best question" was the saying and this one fit. "Because the fates meant for the tacks to stay wedged due to the horrific behavior of the shoe owner." (In other words, the tacks stayed in place because he deserved to die.)

Poisons were at Dad's core. I recognized the Jimson weed at the cabin with my knowledge from Dad. I knew of the Manchineel and the Poisonwood, plentiful Florida plants, both deadly. Nightshade, Monkshood, Hellebores: These he knew intimately and shared with me. I fell the box might contain poison, administered to the victim in a way that necessitated the box remaining sealed, a trap of some sort.

I folded the note up and began to read the book. I found a poem entitled "My Test" which read:
"When tragedy like this comes to thee,
'Tis for some reason and a test for thine own soul,
To build a finer thing,
Possessed of something deeper, more divine,
Preparing thee to pay thy toll to Father
Time;
And, he, the keeper of the records
Passes by."
In light pencil he had written "It's for that hardest travail. Use wisely and once."

The box was to be opened but one time, what happened after that would extract me from my deepest trouble. And suddenly the puzzle slipped into clarity, like the final piece of the jigsaw. My father was saying "This was 'no alabaster box.'"

He would have enjoyed the irony of finding just the right book of poetry with just the right title to clothe his clue. How literal it was. It became one more of his adages, strictly by happenstance.

* * *

My prison guard work was surprisingly easy. I blended in because I did what a redneck prison guard would do—kept my mouth shut, obeyed orders, and quickly became known as a good paperwork doer. I began in the stamping shop where license plates were manufactured. Twenty inmates under the watch of four of us. The other three guards were white, all in their twenties, all crackers. Glade Honninger was my "partner". We looked out for each other, especially one another's back. "Hind yo," meant "behind you," i.e., an inmate had made a suspicious move and to be careful. It was barked out like a marine sergeant's order. The stamping shop inmates had earned the right to be there. It was considered higher up on the work ladder than the roadwork detail or the gravel pit work. This latter in particular was considered hard labor. You could lose your stamping work if you did something wrong and got demerits. Then you'd go down the ladder to gravel or lower, still, solitary.

Higher above stamping plates, you moved into "trusty" jobs: laundry, postal work, library work, household jobs for the warden's family.

The supervisor was a black man, Isaac Coleman. He weighed in at 250 and was known as "Big Eye". He nephew Isaac Blackledge was a guard and was known as "Little Eye". He weighed in at 200, so size was certainly not the criterion. Must have been rank. I took my knapsack to work. In it was the box and the book. I kept the sack locked in my car trunk.

Glade I grew to like. I had no friends growing up, and George was like a father or favorite uncle to me, but Glade and I hit it off. He had a young wife Lu and they had me over for a home-cooked meal a time or two. I reciprocated by meeting them at a restaurant down DeFuniak way. I did not relish disclosing my living arrangements with anyone. I had stopped at the Peaceton tax office, found the cabin had several years of back tax owing and was on a list for tax foreclosure. But the taxes on the cabin were low; the amount due was $482.00. I paid that up, had the electricity turned on and began picking up a few furnishings at yard sales. My life was settling into a routine, and I found I was actually enjoying it.

"If you're running, run like the rabbit," my Dad had said. He meant when you run, run scared. Keep your adrenaline on the up. Look at everyone as a potential enemy or a betrayer to an enemy, whether intended or not. Do not let your guard down. Do not relax too much; that's when you'll do or say something that'll give you away. These thoughts kept running through my mind as I patrolled the stamping presses each day.

At the end of the first month I called George as planned. He caught me up on events back in New Rochelle. Sonny had stewed around town about how he'd been hooked out of his money by me, he'd get revenge, etc, etc, etc.

But in the end the goods against him were too strong. He was forced to plead out. He pled to a lesser charge and had jail time of five years, but George said that with time off for good behavior it would end up as two years or so. He had crooked judges who owed his crime family big time and things would go his way. My chips were one dead mother, one father in prison without crime family connections, and no known relatives on either side with a modicum of influence. Not much on my side except $50,000 of this bastard's money!

A year went by, and I watched the seasons pass in the highest, most northerly edge of Florida. People have said there are no weather changes in Florida, but the Panhandle does in fact have seasons. One event did occur during that year which could be connected to my father's arcane knowledge of poisons.

There was a trusty named Drift Anstruther who worked in the kitchen. This was a plum job with a lot of perks. He was allowed to smoke, he could take extra food for himself, you get the picture—a good deal all 'round. He handled incoming food shipments which included a good deal of contraband which he sold to the inmates including marijuana and some cocaine. He'd never been caught outright at any of this. His sexual bent was of the tough homosexual variety. He had a stable of two or three pets called gunsels who got extra treats for servicing Drift's needs. One day Little Eye finally got wind of this and he and Big Eye beat Drift with rubber truncheons and left him in a heap on the kitchen floor. That evening was garbage collection pick up. The garbage was taken to a neighborhood piggery run by the institution and staffed by trustys. Drift had curled up in one of the garbage barrels and gone out in the collection truck. He apparently dropped off the truck at a stop sign at a turn on little used road in the woods and disappeared. By ten that night the escape siren was sounding, and I was part of a posse looking for him. We scoured the woods within a ten-mile radius. Glade Honninger and I spent a good part of the night canvassing the nooks and crannies of an old phosphate mine close by. The barbed wire which had surrounded it had long rusted out and the brush had reclaimed it as its own. We had a pack of hounds with us, but it was dark and dangerous work—sudden drop-offs and holes that could break a horse's leg. By dawn we'd pretty well covered it and went to a central command post which had been set up. All posse members were back except the two Isaacs. Nowhere to be found. Almost an hour passed before they hove in, looking none the worse for wear, but not being the usual font of volubility—their usual mien. I had a feeling something was up, but what I didn't know.

Next the statewide search went out—the usual "escaped convict on the loose" bit. The Georgia, Alabama, and Mississippi police were also alerted since we were so close to the state bounds. Nothing came back from this until two days later. A camper from a campground not five miles away was out hiking and found what was left of Drift. He had been tied to a Manchineel tree. The sap which is vitriolic and copious had run down the trunk, burning him and pickling and flaying the flesh from him. Death had been slow and horrible. He was buried face down, his mouth filled with dirt and his lips sown together in order that he not be called forth from his grave as a Zombie following Voodoo folklore. I supposed Big Eye and Little Eye were perhaps superstitious about this.

So that was what Manchineel could do. It left me with a much greater awareness of my Dad's knowledge, but more than that, his power. There was a creepy eerieness to it, but an awe as well. Like finding out your father was Merlin. Why did he know these things? Everyone else's father wasn't like this. I felt like I was skirting along the edge of the paranormal, although I didn't know that word until later in my self-education, I felt a little off balance by witnessing the results to Drift Anstruther. Unnerved.

Another year later, an event happened which caused my easy-going life in Peaceton to change. I had been shifted in the work ladder to Orientation officer. This meant I handled the daily inflow of many new prisoners to the institution. Luckily for me, I did not meet the new inductees right away. Coden Hosford who worked with me did that. He was a very young twenty-two year old with the over serious attitude of the "person in charge", a bit overly in love with his own power. My office door had a transom which allowed me to hear two new arrivals in the waiting room. The list showed two northerners who'd been picked up in an attempted "hit" of a New York businessman over on the Atlantic coast, who'd incurred heavy gambling debts and couldn't pay. I hopped onto my desk and peered through the transom: Rocco Volterra and Bart "Little Pup" Porpora, two hoods I'd see around Sonny Lupo's old haunts. I glanced down at the nameplate pinned to my shirt "Egils Rushing" it said in caps. They might not recognize me by face but that tag . . . time to remove myself. I ducked out the side entry to the processing building, stopped by "Big Eye's" office and told him my grandmother was real sick and I had to go. I drove back up to the cabin, took a few items of clothing and headed out of town. Where to go? Here I had been sure I was hidden in plain sight and bam! There was my past in the damn processing building ready to send word back to Lupo. Then it hit me; I'd driven right by it coming across Florida from the East coast—Chattahoochee. The loony bin. Now, surely no hoods from up North were going to go crazy and end up in a Florida funny farm. This time it seemed foolproof: hide in plain sight.

Talking my way into an aide's job at the Florida State Hospital was easy with my prior work experience as a prison guard. I told then I needed to switch to work nearer a sick grandmother, and they accepted this and asked no questions. I phoned Big Eye and said I would have to quit my job there for the same reason. Hang onto my last paycheck—I'd pick it up in a few weeks when things settled down with Granma, I slept in a motel a few nights while I scouted a new place to live. I read the local obituaries and found the death of a ninety year old with children in their sixties who obviously were settled elswhere. I hung around the dead lady's house each evening for a few days after work. Sure enough by the fifth evening, a car with North Carolina plates was parked in the driveway. The Lepells were retirees from an assisted living facility in Asheville, North Carolina. They had tried for years, they told me, to pry his mother out of her house into a similar situation, but she had stubbornly resisted. That sort of living was not widely available in the Panhandle at that time and she didn't want to leave her neighbors and her daily routine. The house was frozen in time at about 1949, and she was totally happy with it. I offered a good rent. I said it was fine to leave the furniture. Take what they wanted no problem. The house was perfect. A thirties bungalow an easy walk from the hospital.

I was off one afternoon about two weeks later. I went back over to the correctional center to pick up my last paycheck. I cashed it in Peaceton and drove over to the cabin to pick up a few things. The inside was not trashed, but someone had definitely been there. The rear window to the kitchen in the lean-to was left open where entry had been made. The mattress was upended, every kitchen article examined and misplaced, desk rifled, coffee pot searched and left on its side, refrigerator slightly moved, toilet tank fished through, a professional job. I took what I came for and left it exactly as I'd found it. If they (he) came back, what little I took wouldn't be missed. I did not want it known that I'd been there. Lupo or a henchman had discovered my lair. It had been a close call, and I needed to talk to George.

I left Peaceton double-time and drove back to

Chattahoochee. I called George from a payphone in Marianna. George had often called me back on this payphone.

Two things I learned from George: 1) Sonny Lupo was out and 2) I mentioned the break-in to George and said could he figure out any way Sonny could've glommed onto the Panhandle as a possible hideout for me. Turned out George hadn't received his office phone bill the past month and had had to get a duplicate from the phone company. First time in twenty years this had ever happened. There were two returned calls from George's office number to a payphone I'd often used in Peaceton. We both knew . . .

I told George I wouldn't call again for a while. It was getting too risky.

The next few days I weighed a run to a totally different part of the country, say Texas or California. But I thought better of it. Sonny would likely assume I'd do something like that. He had Mafia eyes to look throughout the country for me. "Hide in plain sight," kicked in again, and I truly thought my loony bin cover was a good one.

I came to enjoy being an aide, far more than correctional work. It meant I was helping people. I was ministering to people which tied in with my mom's nursing and behind her, that long line tracing back to a time of priests and priestesses, seers and soothsayers. Aides could administer meds then, so I did that, and I worked with several elderly patients who were true lifers—too old and far gone to ever return to the outside either because of physical infirmity or totally blown mentality. They had been abandoned by their families, left to die alone. Many were harmless but lonely, and only wanted a kind word or a short bull session.

This is a good time to bring up my dad yet one more time.

Dad was handsome. That word doesn't begin to convey it, the Indian bearing, the piercing gaze that penetrated you and went beyond to eternity. His high cheekbones. The straight up stance. The movement of him: panther-like, hardly touching the ground. He crept up on you. You looked up suddenly and he was there. His visage was feline, delicate-feminine looking, yet just missing effeminacy. And slightly dangerous looking, too, pointed sideburns and slightly reddish curly black hair that curled about his ears and ended in a swirl point in the middle of the back of his neck. He had tight ears, faun-like. And women always sensed what lay between his legs. It was a treasure waiting to get out, granpa said. Once I was standing in the bar of the Mercury looking out the window at nothing in particular and Dad hove into view walking down the street. There was a slight backward movement to his walk, not a slouch because his back was arrow straight but as though his panther prowl feet came first and the upper part of his torso and head were following a fraction behind, kind of riding on air-waves that his walk created. I have never seen another man who walked like that—"mince" or "prance" has too much leg lifting to do it, maybe "meech" (Definitively an Alicia word, and one I'd never heard or knew of till much later).

Anyhow a middle aged woman passing him going the opposite way never got her eyes above his belt buckle, kept going and went on with her head so swiveled devouring what she'd just seen and rather seriously injured herself when she walked hard into a fire hydrant and smacked over. I couldn't believe she hadn't broken her thighbone when she hit. She was in shorts and had a bruise there that must have lasted all summer—that was Dad.

I tell you this because, not that I had his exquisite looks, but I was his son. Let's leave it there.

Women had been attracted to me from puberty on. My growing up years had been solitary ones, sports were beginning to be out of town budgets, and I therefore had no locker room experience of nakedness, no comparisons to others; even standing at a urinal modesty kicked in. I could "go" without fully unreeling it full length from my underpants.

After the barn incident some of the stuff the other guys had said up to then made more sense I had been called "Bone" and "Woody" and not known why.

But for all this my Dad's "keep yourself to yourself" I took literally, like everything else. I would go to marriage a virgin and did. That's what it meant to me. In fact my disillusionment over Dad came as corollary when his "career" surfaced. I felt he'd broken his own commandment. He hadn't kept himself to himself.

I took night hours as much as possible. I liked it. I

was single, all the female aides were single moms, so I was looked upon as a god-send. The ward was quiet at night. Sleeping pills and Thorazine kept it still and peaceful, peaceful and still. Paper work was always easy for me. I was speedy and efficient at it. I read a good part of each night I was on duty. I lapped up book-learning like a hungry sponge. And my vocabulary. I'd gotten the idea that how one spoke was the single most powerful tool to rising through the American class structure, and I meant to rise. If I ever got out of this mess I found myself in. I read all of Keats (the bravest of men), the convoluted patterns of Hawthorne, father and son. The pagan cruelty and spareness of Robinson Jeffers appealed mightily to me. Something unusual: the hospital library had a full (I guess) set of the old novels of Basil King. I read them all. There was a sanctimonious primness there, true, but the plot lines were intriguing; the "fixes" his characters got in; the early twentieth century was the era of the good plot— no sex, but stories and good ones.

So life settled to a quiet routine. Good nursing work and good learning work.

And then Carla Rhodes arrived—Carla was a classic Southern beauty—perfect features, allicient raven hair, long and silky beautiful legs, also long and silky arched eyebrows over big blue eyes. The blue was startling with the back hair and white skin. She looked at you the way a malamute husky stares. She'd come out of a cracker town near Jacksonville. She'd won numerous beauty contests. Then, age about twenty eight, bi-polar Carla started coming through. She was arrested several times for shoplifting; then she stole a car down near Delray. She almost got jail-time for that one. Then she ended up in a psycho ward in Orlando for a suicide attempt. She was diagnosed there and put on lithium. It made her fat, she said, so she'd quit the meds periodically and trouble would begin again. A lengthy stay at a private clinic pushed her mother to the brink of bankruptcy. Finally nothing left for Carla but Chattahoochee, after another attempt at suicide.

I didn't see her until she'd come out of the psycho ward. It was felt she could be in the general hospital population as long as her medication was monitored. We had tricks to be sure the meds were swallowed. You had to drink a full glass of water, we'd grip the back of the neck to force the patient to swallow without thinking.

Female personnel had been working with Carla, but a mild flu epidemic put us short-handed. That's when I got my first encounter. I was wearing my usual work garb, white scrub top and tie pants. She came to the dispensary to get her meds and saw me standing there with a tiny paper cup and the pills. She stared at me, starting at my face but moving down and riveting at my hips. "Will you look at you, honey; got you a jelly roll in there? Wantin' to play in my playpen, huh?"

I stood straight still and handed her the cup. Water came next and I saw her swallow. Suddenly she had the string of my pants and I turned quickly totally around. Another aide, Monica Musgrave came in just then.

"That's enough of that, Carla. I heard you way out in the hall talkin' dirty like that. Keep that up and you'll have to go back to the unit." I just said, "Thanks, Monica." I went back through the door to the hall. I knew I didn't want to make a big thing out of it. It would only cause attention to focus on me. I also knew I needed to stay far, far away from Carla in future. She was too volatile and might accuse me of rape or assault. "Keep yourself to yourself." I asked the supervisor to be removed from duty involving Carla Rhodes, and he agreed.

Four months later I was on day shift. Shift broke at three, and I had a few errands to do. I caught an early flick and it was getting dark when I pulled into the driveway. For some reason (I finally remembered later in piecing it all together that it was because I had two grocery bags in my arms) I put the knapsack through my arms rather than carrying it by the straps like I usually did. I entered the kitchen and put the two bags down on the countertop. I had turned on the overhead fluorescent light with its doughnut shaped bulb.

Suddenly I felt just the faintest trace of movement. I whirled around, I heard the snap of the kitchen light switching off, a huge intense pain in my head and darkness.

I was swimming in a wine-dark sea of deep purple almost black. There were kaleidoscope whirling pinpoints of light, like children made when they swirl sparklers. Then I felt very heavy like I wasn't going to swim any more, I was going to drown in this delicious dark purple wine. But it was OK this wonderful drowning whirlpool, and then I was under an overhead garage door. It was very heavy and I was trying to push it up. I pushed and pushed and I was awake. It was dark, but I could see objects around me in the dark space, spare tire, tire iron, snow scraper... I was on my side, and my hands were tied in front of me, miraculously the knapsack still on my back. I could feel the hard lump of the box in the small of my back. The sack had probably been too time-consuming and unwieldy to remove from a limp, dead weight. So they had left it. I was moving, I could feel that, a pretty straight road, not a lot of curves. I felt we were traveling westerly—don't know why. I could hear the fast swoosh as we crossed a bridge, and the rhythmic click if we hit a stretch paved with concrete blocks. I began to get more alert and pieced together other clues. The trunk was large. It had to be a big American car. The presence of the snow scraper indicated the car was from the North. The only person with a grudge was Sonny Lupo. Sonny often drove a black Lincoln Towncar. We crossed what I felt was a long bridge, then slowed down and turned to the left. The car stopped, then I heard only one door slam. Evidently Sonny was alone. This grudge was a personal one not connected to Mafia business, so he had likely been told he was on his own. The trunk opened, and there was my nemesis in the flesh. He had painstakingly tracked me down, and I lay there like a trussed pig. It was dark, probably the midnight range judging from the length of the ride from Chattahoochee. The .45 was gleaming in the pale moonlight and the seductive extra length of the silencer was noticeable as he pulled me from the trunk and half dragged me across the filthy yard. I wondered if the silencer was one of Dad's. The irony of that slipped across my consciousness like the faint whisper of a bat's wing. I could see several ramshackle metal sheds and steel animal traps stacked up in a pile. One pen had several muzzled thin dogs pacing back and forth—they appeared to be greyhounds. We approached a large cylinder lying on its side. A small hatch-door was cut into the end. A gauge was visible, and I began to fear the worst. It looked like something could be pumped or let into the interior—something probably lethal.

"You fucking bastard" Sonny snarled. "you can run but you can't hide."

He opened the hatch and lifting me up like a limp rag, threw me inside.

"See what this will do to soften you up you smartass punk," he shut the hatch, I heard the click of a padlock. A few minutes later I looked up at the top of one of the rounded sides of the cylinder. A hissing noise began. I could see a misty vapor issuing from a small pipe set in the top of the side, a sickly sweet odor began to fill the cylinder. It smelled of bubblegum, I remember, but sweeter than that, cloying sinuous and finally nauseous. I twisted and turned trying to escape from this overpowering fog enveloping me, a sickening cloud of sleepiness and death.

Then I slumped over into darkness.

I didn't die. How long I lay there I don't know. It had to be two days from the growth of beard I could feel on my face. My hands were still tied in the front, a mistake on Sonny's part, but likely caused by the knapsack interfering with tying me across my back. He probably felt rushed doing all this in my kitchen, afraid of being spotted by a neighbor and wanting to get me out of there fast.

I spent my time trying to rub the rope against something sharp enough to fray. Little luck—the interior of my prison was empty and totally smooth.

My mood swings swung wildly between two poles. "Let him have the money" was one pole. "It'll do you no good if you're dead. Work a deal that if he'll let me go he can have the money—all of it."

The second pole was "No way. Not only did he murder my mother as sure as if he'd shot her dead, he'll never let me go. I know too much and he blames me, in his primitive Sicilian mindset, for putting him in prison and taking his money."

Pole two began to loom large in the overall scheme of things.

The lump in my backpack was rubbing between my shoulder blades. The plan was set. Almost as though the box was talking to me.

Time passed. I began wondering if The Wolf was not coming back. I could die in this crazy cylinder and never be found. This dismal prospect became more insistent to me. Adrenaline started pumping I had to get out of the cylinder or die trying.

Just then the hatch opened and Sonny poked his head in, "You ready to squeal thieving schieve?"

"Look Sonny" I said. "I'll give you the frigging dough. Just untie me and I'll get it for you."

"That's a good one" he muttered "but no funny stuff." Waving his gun at me, he pulled me out of the cylinder hatch and I fell onto the filthy ground. He pulled the strands of polyester rope apart enough to shoot the rope between my two hands. The silencer made the sound "thwup" as my two arms flew apart from the sudden release of pressure.

I fell back from the suddenness of my release and the back straps of the sack fell down and the canvas fell to the ground beside me.

"Here," I said pulling out the box. I have said it was hard to hold onto. The corners were all rounded. It looked like a loaf of store-bought Wonderbread. The silvery glint sparkled in the moonlight,

"Here, the bank book is in here" as I handed it to him. "I've sealed it with sealing wax to keep it from opening apart. Have you got a lighter or a match? You can melt it off to open it." He put the gun down on the ground at his feet.

Sonny looked kind of puzzled at the box. He had obviously never seen anything remotely resembling it (and neither had I for that matter).

He, too, had trouble holding it, it was awkward in its shape. He managed to grasp it tightly in one hand holding the top and bottom, and applying heat from a lighter to the sealant girding the middle like a band of wax. It began to bubble and drip off. He had to shift the box to melt off the side bands and then the rear.

It was then that the box began to open apart and the first part of the diabolically clever design of the box became suddenly apparent.

"Yeow!" Sonny yelled; the edges of the opening were razor-sharp, cutting one hand at the tender spot between his thumb and forefinger on the hand holding it. He dropped the box and sucked the blood gushing from his hand. I was paralyzed with fear and wonderment as to what was going to happen next. I had to keep him interested in continuing to open the box. If he threw it down in disgust now that he was bleeding, all would be lost.

"Oh God" I screamed "Not the jewels, the money, yes, ok, but not the jewels." I don't know why I said "jewels". It just flew out of my mouth.

I had to appeal to his cupidity. It worked.

"Wha' da fuck. Jewels in dere?" He pulled the other side of the box open with his other hand and the razor edges did their work there as well.

Bleeding profusely from both hands he held the box wide open. The moonlight flickered across the contents.

A gorgeous icy glint of diamonds shone outward as I stood there awestruck. Sonny was struck dumb as well. The necklace lay in a contoured circle at the bottom of the box, one huge stone forming the center.

Both his hands dripping he thrust them inside to pick up the treasure. His face was agleam with an animal grimace. His mouth was pulled back around his teeth. The Wolf was in for the kill and the necklace was the prize. The chief stone was affixed to the contoured inset which held it and as he pulled it he screamed in agony. A steel spike was hidden beneath the stone, so slippery from his blood it impaled itself onto the hand wresting the necklace from its resting place. It worked like a fishhook and thoroughly imbedded itself and the box with it to his hand.

He began writhing, trying to extract the box from his punctured hand. As he hit the box against the outside wall of the cylinder I saw a shatter of glass. Not diamonds . . . glass. Exploding in a candent shower. The ruse was almost complete. The glass stones contained vitriol which covered his hands, flaying the skin from the bone, exposing the muscles and tendons of his hands and another shatter splashed vitriol into his eyes and face. I managed to kick the gun into the tall marsh grass nearby and watched the throes of the fatally injured Sonny.

Wild with pain and terror he blindly staggered away from me. A metal shed lay sullenly gleaming in the moonlight. Sonny hit it in his blindness. The box finally flew from his hand as he hit the shed. He lay writhing, no longer recognizable as a human being, but as a mound of putrefying flesh, blood, muscle and bone.

I noticed for the first time that my holding prison

adjoined a yellowish brown bay of water. The moon had arisen over the bay.

Too horrified to touch the box, I managed with the toe of my boot to inch it towards the water's edge. Gradually I moved it along to the bank and gave it one hefty kick. It flew off the bank with a heavy "clunk" and disappeared. Seething fluid bubbled like a witch's cauldron for several seconds. Then all was silent.

I left the body of Sonny splayed awkwardly where he'd fallen and ran for cover in the neighboring field.

The dirt banks around the field had revealed a hideous secret. I was in a dog graveyard where hundreds, maybe thousands of greyhounds had been killed and buried when no longer able to run at the numerous Florida dog-tracks. Piles of bones stacked up in rows of perfect order. Stacks of sequent feet, each atop the other in a grisly tableau of the macabre. I panicked at the grue surrounding me everywhere and blindly ran, hoping to find a way out this pit of pestilence and horror.

Finally, I found the dirt track out to the highway. I had walked no more than a half mile when I crossed a bridge across the bay where I'd been. A sign said Leaving Alabama, another said Welcome to the Sunshine State. I was on Rt. 98 West of Pensacola. I walked into Pensacola before I hitched a lift. I didn't want to be seen anywhere near the dead-dog pit and the body of Sonny the Wolf Lupo.

That was all to be a mystery of someone else's solving . . .

I holed up for a few days to get myself back on an even keel. I needed to think

It might take months for Sonny's body to be found. The Mafia had considered his feud with me as a personal one. Therefore, I was free of worry on that score. The money was finally mine, and my mother's death was avenged and my own life saved by the handiwork of my father. I felt vindicated. I no longer had reason to hide. I could leave Chattahoochee a free man.

I quit the job at the hospital, mailed the house key to the Lepells and drove east toward the Atlantic coast. Near Palm Beach I picked up a local paper. In the "Help Wanted" section I saw a small ad:

Male attendant wanted to assist male stroke patient. Hospital experience a plus. Personable attitude a must.

My nursing background had provided me with the highest degree of self-satisfaction I had ever experienced. I enjoyed the intellectual expansion it had provided me.

Alicia Salisbury answered the telephone when I called to schedule an interview. She told me immediately I was speaking into a deaf modified speaker. We arranged to meet the following day. If that went well, I was to meet her father. I was struck by the soft pleasant sound of her voice, the tentative quality that her deafness imparted. I sensed a quietness, a charming reserve.

The next morning I drove down to Palm Beach and soon found the Salisbury house. It was a medium sized Spanish house with a tiled rood on one of the quiet side streets just north of the town center. I was ushered into a rear glass enclosed patio, lush with tropical flowering bushes and trees. Theron Salisbury watched my arrival from his wheel chair. His speech was badly impaired, and he had a look of one deeply troubled. Alicia was standing beside him as I entered. Tall, she exuded an air of dignity, grace and an aloofness which was not unfriendly, but due to her inherent shyness. Her affliction fed further into this. She had a way of turning her head sideways as I spoke. She lip read whatever I said. It reminded me of a swan arching its long neck to better see your approach.

"Our telephone conversation yesterday was quite positive, I felt, and so I wanted you to meet my father without further ado," she smiled. Her pale blonde hair was swept away from her face and pinned up in the back by an intricate turquoise comb. Perfectly arched eyebrows framed her large dark eyes and curved lashes. I was beholding a goddess, and I knew it. She motioned me to a seat. Tea was served, and I quietly regarded my new patient. I knew this interview was already going well and that I would be spending much time in this quiet oasis. Terms were easily arranged, and I was to move into an in-law wing of the house with its own kitchen, living room and two bedrooms, one occupied by Theron and I, the other. I was to start the next day. I drove back up the coast to my motel to collect my clothes and *No Alabaster Box*. It had become a talisman for me; I felt it had saved my life along with the box itself now lying in the oozy mud of Perdido Bay. I called George, finally feeling free to talk to him openly without fear of anyone tracing the call.

George had news, lots of it. The Secaucus property had become suddenly valuable. The discount malls were coming in. The house, tavern and barn were perfectly sited for high-volume traffic. George had an offer for $500,000 in cash. The Rosevears were restive. They had saved enough money to buy a place of their own and had found something in Rockaway. They had asked to be released from their lease. I told George to sell and hung up.

My life with the Salisburys was soon settled into a lazy desultory routine. I appreciated this after my fugitive existence in the Panhandle. I found a short piece in the paper about where I'd been held. The property had been raided by the state police who'd been tipped off concerning the burials there. They'd discovered thousands of dog bones, laid in piles and then bulldozed over. The owner had been arrested for animal cruelty. No mention of Sonny. I was sure the owner had buried his remains amongst the dogs and sold the Lincoln.

Mr. Salisbury, who I rapidly began to think of, and call, Theron, was instinctively the grave quiet man whose traits were mirrored in his daughter, Alicia. His speech was badly affected by the stroke. After a few weeks, he began to trust me. Because I sensed he wanted to confide in me, I began to construct a sign language between him and me to augment his stammering attempts at communication. I would wheel him on long walks along the seacoast promenades and boardwalks. Sometimes Alicia would accompany us, sometimes not.

The man was a treasure: kind, considerate, highly moral. A man among men. I looked up to him as a superior being, one I wished to emulate. He never complained about his afflictions, but took them as a matter of course. A stoic, carrying the load that fate had placed upon him

He was titular head of his aircraft manufactory, although no longer able to attend to the business. The day-to-day affairs were in the hands of Alicia and a cousin, Alec Hidell (he carried the title of comptroller). I met Hidell at the end of the first week when he came by to meet with Alicia and Theron. A thin, spare man with a mane of gray hair and a trim moustache, he was clad in pinstripes even in the Florida sun. His overall appearance was too sleek for my taste with his too many rings and heavy gold I.D. bracelet. A man to watch, I thought, and watch I did.

I always discreetly left the three of them alone when he came, but, as time wore on, I noted the increasing look of unease in Theron's eyes, the droop of his shoulders each time Alec left and a distinct hint of frisson in Alicia's manner when his name arose in conversation. (Another Alicia word again, but nothing better conveys it.)

A few days after one of Hidell's visits, I found Theron wheeled up to his desk in his bedroom poring over spreadsheets and figures. Stroke victims often cry unexpectedly in times of great stress. Tears were streaming down Theron's face. I went to him and held him from behind, my arms across his shaking shoulders. His eyes were saying, "can I tell you?" I sensed his reluctance to involve me in his troubles. But understand, I had bathed this man, dressed him, attended to his bathroom needs. What was left between us? I signed our sign for "go on it's ok."

He indicated he was in a terrible quandary. He felt unable to involve Alicia in his morass. He was embarrassed at this inability to control the situation. Hidell was over-reaching his authority and some irregularities in the business accounts were occurring. A goodly number of sums were being paid to two corporate entities, Norec, Inc. and Cixot, Inc. Hidell kept insisting these were consulting firms he had hired to help in finding a buyer for the company and that it was money well spent. The sums were mounting and Theron's tears were those of frustration at his lack of control. Add to this, the beginnings of suspicion which was casting a shadow. Suspicion of embezzlement? So it seemed to me.

Theron's confiding in me put me in a delicate situation vis-à-vis Alicia. Heretofore, this woman had been his soul mate, his alter ego, from whom he kept nothing. The two had led two connate lives until I had entered.

Till now, however, he had always been the captain at the helm of his company. Alicia was the sounding board often in company problems, but the ultimate power had been Theron's. And Alicia had never desired that it be any other way.

Therefore, I felt that I had no choice but to express Theron's concerns to his daughter and to do so with all speed. I said to Theron, "Let me take this on for you. Let me handle the telling of this to Alicia" I added "it could well be that Alicia already has an inkling of your suspicions, may know quite a bit in fact."

He indicated relief that it had been taken off his back, and that I might be able to help him.

Things rapidly came to pass that I was needed sooner rather than later. An offer to purchase the company arrived directly to Theron from people whom he knew from business. It was from a large conglomerate with many holdings in the defense industry. The sum was princely for its time, $5 million. The letter of intent stipulated that the Salisbury family was not to sell or encumber any of their stock in the company prior to the closing of sale. This was of importance because if there was any malfeasance, it had to be remedied by Salisbury assets other than company stock. It meant Alicia and Theron stood to lose hundreds of thousands if Cixot and Norec were shells for Hidell's filchings.

Theron had retired early the night the offer had arrived. There was an air of electricity in the atmosphere. Alicia was sitting on the back veranda behind the house looking at the stars. I stepped out from the in-law wing I shared with her father and said,

"I am not anxious to interfere in any way between you and your father. He is immensely worried about Hidell and fears there is bad mischief with the books.

You and I need to find out, or this sale to Golconda Holding won't go through. There may be as much as half a million at stake here."

She looked as though I had struck her. Her face froze, her lovely eyes stared at me, "I knew there's been something wrong, so wrong these past weeks. This had been going on for so long, long before you came. It's been eating away at him, slowly defeating him, oh he's so weak now and helpless and tired" she put her head into her hands just as a small child would, hiding the tears that coursed down into her lap. "I can't help him, that is what is killing me, it's too much for me. I'm not strong enough for Alec. He's been a bully to me since I was a child. He's clever and cruel and oh so smart and he's insinuated himself into the company and our lives and he's traded on being part of my father's family and used it to his own ends and devices." This tumble of words came out in a torrent, as though long pent up and now suddenly released,

"So you knew this was possible," I said softly.

"Oh yes." she looked up into my face. "But he was so clever about it all, so slippery, and he had Dad fooled I think; he was always so clever with figures and in his early time at the company he seemed to make some of Dad's pressing problems go away as though by magic, Dad grew to rely on him, after all he was family, don't you know. And now I'm wondering if there are other things he might have put Dad's name to, and our name dragged into the mud, it's all too horrible." She looked at me like a wounded bird, a yellow canary with a broken wing, and I wanted to hold her and kiss her and make it all better again, but I hadn't earned that right yet. I was but the servant, the attender of the master, and it wasn't my place.

Heart-broken I could but bow, look into her eyes and quietly utter: "Let me look into this for you. I can work quietly without Hidell finding out. The plant is up in Bangor, isn't it? Can you spare me for a few days?"

"Oh yes, Gil." She'd not used my Christian name before, only Mr. Rushing.

"Oh if you could only help us. You'd save our lives and Dad's honor . . ."

"Oh yes I could and I will, M'Lady," I thought to myself, and I suddenly saw the lithograph of the holy grail tacked to the wall in the lowly Rushing cabin back in Peaceton. The Quest of the San Graal. Now I knew what adoration was all about. I was experiencing it.

I quietly bowed and left her.

The next morning found me flying to Boston and then Bangor. I rented a car and drove to Salisbury Manufacturing, Inc., outside Bangor.

It was a typical New England type of enterprise. The buildings, five in all, had formerly housed a log-turning mill back in the early Maine heyday. I had the keys to Theron's office and, more importantly, Alec Hidell's office as well. Unless he'd had the locks changed—but no, he'd likely felt secure enough not to bother. Theron was certainly not going to trouble him, and Alicia hadn't been to the plant in over a year.

Security was one night watchman, Silas Haslam, with a drinking problem. There were no security issues throughout Maine at this particular time, so Silas was probably superfluous except for one security issue, namely me.

I parked the car on a side road—I was dressed entirely in black, black gloves, black navy watch cap pulled down over my hair. One of the five plant buildings was nudged up against a weed-covered hillside topped by a copse of fir trees. I waited in the copse until I spotted Silas making his rounds. He lurched past my building, and the coast was clear. The barbed wire fence ran behind the building, but was actually below me due to the sharp incline of the hill. I easily jumped across the fence right onto the backside roof of the building and slid down a drainpipe to the ground. The next building housed the administrative offices. I slipped in. So far so good. Alicia's description had been perfect.

The secretary's desk was outside Hidell's inner office, and on it my flash light disclosed some mail which hadn't yet made it to his attention. A bank statement with cancelled checks. And there lay in my hand a check for $5,000 payable to Cixot, Inc. Signed by A. J. Hidell. On the reverse side it had been endorsed by Cixot, Inc for deposit only, a blurred name beneath that looked purposely unreadable, but deposited into an account at the Bank of Boca Raton. Now we were getting somewhere! I replaced the check, resealed the envelope and left it on the desk. I saw Silas wheeling by again with the alcoholic "listing to starboard" gait. I slipped from the building, shimmied up the drain to the adjacent roof and was back into the copse of trees and then to Bangor Airport. I registered at the Airport Motel and was out of Bangor and heading back to Palm Beach the following morning . . .

Now to find Cixot in Boca Raton. I suspected Hidell was using a mail drop for Cixot's bank statements. Boca Raton is a hot bed of this sort of activity. It contains every mail fraud, con-artist, sleazy product known to man. The slickest tabloids are published here. It is the Den of 40 Thieves of America (though housing far more than forty.)

The next morning I was dressed as a telephone repairman and walked into the Bank of Boca Raton. I wore tight jeans, a bulging black tee shirt and had a phone mouthpiece hanging from my belt and a hardhat on my head. Dark shades finished it off, and I strode over to a desk on the main floor. Behind it sat a heavily made-up doxy with henna red hair with blue highlights and three earring hoops per ear. I pretended to have a wad of gum in my mouth and said.

"Hey bootiful help me out here, I finished puttin' that phone in on two, and my next work order is for sumpin' called Cixot. My office can't find the address. You got it by chance?"

Her eyes devoured my crotch and what lay inside. She was mesmerized like the mouse ready for the snake to take her whole. She would have used her desktop if I'd have let her.

"Uh . . . sure" she finally blushed "You spell it?"

"C-I-X-O-T" say I as she types it into her computer, "dumb name huh?"

"39 Bedson St. Suite A." She gulps still immersed in my nether regions.

"Tanks" say I making a smacking noise like popping gum.

"You free tonight?" says red haired Annie.

"Not to you, honey, not to you" and I'm already through the door.

By the time she's back from fantasyland and has realized she's just committed a rather major security breach, I'm turning into Bedson Street, a short side street off the main drag of Boca Raton. 39 is one of a series of tired three storey mixed-use stucco 1950's buildings. No elevator, just dingy stairwells; the denizens of this lowlife world include finance companies, window shade outlets, fourth rate lawyers and accountants, dregsville.

Suite A has Bugloss and Dempster Attorneys-at-Law. Actually, it read "Bulgoss and Dempster _ttorneys-at-La_" with but a faint outline traced onto the door where the "a" and "w" had formerly lived.

My telephone ruse having worked so well, I decided it was worth a reprise. I slouched in swinging my phone again and feeling like I should belt out a chorus of "YMCA," but I foreswore the temptation.

The firm of Messers Bugloss and Dempster looked like it survived on marginal enterprise at best. It had a collection agency corner suitably fenced with an overweight gorgon in attendance behind a screen and three recreants waiting in line to pay up something on account of some sorry little debt—nickel and dime stuff. Mr. Dempster appeared busy in his office closing a usurious second or third mortgage for a couple who reeked of gin all the way out to where I stood. They looked defeated, but thirsty.

Another desk seemed devoted to purveying a line of Miracle Vitamins (maybe Mr. Bugloss was in charge of this department). The far corner office housed a vinyl siding and gutter line called cell-o-texa mirror glo. Should you desire to encase your Florida dream castle in this, you actually got a mirror finish to your siding and gutters so the little wife could primp up while leaving for the evening before she got to the make-up mirror in the car.

I stood a minute looking around at this assortment of oddments and said to no one in particular,

"I'm Ted from the phone company, Mr. Hidell sent me to put in a phone for him. You know what office that'd be?"

Mr. Dempster suddenly moved with startling alacrity from the gin mill his office was rapidly becoming. "What the fuck is Hidell doing . . ." then he caught himself "There's no Hidell in this office. There must be a mistake" this latter all nicely lawyerly and professional with a sibilant "s" in "mistake".

"Wrong building I guess or maybe he meant "Dodson." (another street close by) I stopped slouching and was already swiftly out the door to the hallway as I said this. I had what I wanted: they knew Hidell. I went back to the Salisburys.

Theron was napping, and Alicia was out for the afternoon. I explained to the temporary nurse that I was Theron's regular attendant and that he could take the rest of the afternoon off. He lit up like a Christmas Tree and was gone in thirty seconds.

I typed a letter to Alec Hidell c/o Bugloss and Dempster:

"Your game is up. I know what you're doing. Get out while you still can. One Who Knows."

I sealed it, stamped it and walked to the corner and mailed it.

We needed to stop Hidell's shenanigans before he could steal anymore money. Now we needed to find out how much was gone.

I couldn't resist: on the address I wrote Bugloss and Dumpster.

That night Hilda Grindle, who oversaw the house known as High Keene and who had a set of plant keys as well, met a locksmith there and changed the locks to Hidell's office, Theron's office and the building itself. A guard service was hired to protect the plant and keep Hidell out. Hilda took all the books to High Keene. The corporate accountants began their work and determined how much Hidell had stolen and if there were other shell entities in addition to Cixot and Norec.

"It's Mr. Fernald on the phone," said the maid at the Salisbury house. Theron, Alicia and I were sitting on the veranda. Fernald was the Salisbury accountant.

Alicia picked up the phone, "Hello, Caleb, how bad is it?" she asked.

"It's $500,000. A healthy sum. Luckily it was only the two: Cixot and Norec. The hemorrhaging has stopped at least." Alicia nodded at me and replied, "Thanks to our detective Gil Rushing," she smiled at me.

Alicia and I had a relationship that was now firmly set on a bedrock foundation. She looked upon me as a staunch ally in the thwarting of Hidell and his schemes. She trusted my judgment and my ability to get things accomplished. Plus she appreciated my diplomatic skills in not coming between her and Theron. She sensed that I understood and appreciated her desire to keep the Salisbury name from dishonor and scandal. The Salisburys were a proud race. Their name and reputation were vitally important to them. The Salisburys did not relish victimhood and hated being pitied.

My father's axiom "Pity is always offensive and is generally meant to be so" match their credo exactly.

Caleb Fernald was an old family friend of Theron's early Maine boyhood and had been the Salisbury accountant from the firm's inception.

"Somehow," said Caleb, "You've got to get $500,000 back into the firm account, so we can certify the balances to the Golconda folks and close this deal. We may never see $5 million again and with Theron's health . . ."

"I know, I know," intercepted Alicia sadly. "And

we're strapped right now in not being able to sell or encumber Salisbury stock under the terms of the agreement. Most of our assets are in the Salisbury stock," she added.

Fernald moved on saying, "The defalcation needs to be erased fast. Hidell is loose and could queer the whole deal by saying something to the Golconda people."

By now, Alicia had me listening on an extension. Theron sat in his wheelchair looking alert, but worried. Too much stress right now could kill him I thought. He looked like a wounded eagle, proud upright, but nursing a mortal wound.

He stammered and stuttered in his agitation and finally signed to me, "Life insurance. I have a $500, 000 policy. I'm through."

"No, no, no," screamed Alicia once she understood the gist of his train of thought. "Nothing is worth that, nothing. We'll starve first." She dropped the phone in her excitement. The tears were glistening.

"Your life for my financial independence—never."

My adoration of this sacred creature was complete. I spoke again to Fernald. "There may be another way to do this. Let me take it from here." We all hung up.

Hidell was nowhere to be found. He knew the jig was up. He had $500, 000 of the Salisbury's money. I did wonder how much of a cut he'd had to give Messieurs. Bulgoss and Dempster. It had to have been plenty for providing the drop. At least he was gone. I had other problems to solve.

Thanks to the sale of Secaucus to the mall developers I had $500,000 in my Marianna bank. What better use of it than to bail out the Salisbury's cash flow problem. If I was ever to be the better man I had sought to become all these past years and not just the son of my father, now was the time to show my true colors. Here was Theron willing to fall on his sword to protect his daughter's honor, and the daughter willing to spend a lifetime in penury to preserve her father's. And me in the middle of it all with the money to solve it. I called Fernald and told him money would be wired into the Salisbury firm account within 24 hours. And so it was.

Picture this: the next day father and daughter are placed in the position of financial independence for their lives brought about the hand of a hireling—a man they did not know from Adam not three months ago. He comes from the Chattahoochee Looney Bin and from a nowheresville background and bails out one of the finer families of the American industrial complex. That's a lot to digest.

The Salisburys were up to this digestive process. My star was ascendant at last.

At the end of another three weeks the consolidation of Salisbury Manufacturing Inc. into Golconda Holding Co. was completed. The Salisburys, father and daughter, were free from business worries. Their good name was free of scandal and ridicule. The sum of $500,000 cash was back in my own bank account. That left only Hidell. Something new was evolving in my character since my falling under the influence of the Salisburys. Prior to that, I'd have jumped onto Alec Hidell's trail, found him and possibly killed him. That was the normal pathway to vengeance which I had learned so thoroughly from my Dad and his forebears. I knew Theron and Alicia's first thought would be to let him go, not drag their name into the tabloid press with a trial should he be caught. Perhaps there were better answers than just "vengeance is mine." Maybe I was becoming less primitive under their aegis. I spent a lot of time those next weeks mulling about this. Hidell had done wrong, no doubt. Bringing him before the bar of justice might do more harm than good to his victims. An itch of retribution was gnawing at my soul, but not at theirs. It was all puzzling. I thirsted to learn more.

I spent the next several months working with Theron. I was attempting to bring him back to the land of the living. His had improved and I taught him to speak slowly so as not to panic and fall into stuttering or stammering. We spent the mornings on the veranda which ran along the rear of the house or the patio which adjoined the in-law section. In the afternoons we took long drives or else I pushed his wheelchair in the many seaside parks along the Atlantic coast. Hidell's name was never mentioned, but Theron's gratitude to me in restoring the Salisbury name was spoken of often. Alicia was now a woman of independent means. Her father had settled a goodly percentage of the merger funds upon her. She could now use her own money to help further a line of educational endeavors dear to her heart—training deaf children. A nearby school for the deaf became her bailiwick.

Alicia's own deafness was not a total lack of hearing. As long as she could see the person speaking she could "hear" by a combination of lip reading and partial true hearing. In situations where she couldn't see lips, sometimes she could hear that person, sometimes not. It largely depended upon the timbre of the speaker's voice.

We rarely ate out. The fashionable watering holes of Palm Beach didn't draw Alicia, and Theron was too proud to be seen in public. The Palm Beach house was one from Alicia's mother's family. The naturally reticent quality was strong in both father and daughter, and they were truly happiest when in each other's company. The Palm Beach "scene" was not them.

Alicia's work with the deaf occasionally entailed a trip to the State of Florida School of the Deaf in St. Augustine. She did not like this drive which was a lengthy one up the coast. As I said, my work upon Theron's condition had brought considerable improvement to the point where he could be left for short spells with only the housekeeper in charge.

Alicia was suffering from a bad cold when one of these St. Augustine trips were due. It had settled in her ears which made her fell "dopey", as she put it. It meant being away for most of the day which I had never done before without a temp being brought in. Theron was adamant. "Go with her," he said in his improved speech, "I'll be fine," and he added, "Mrs. Riggins is here all day today till five, and you'll be back by then or shortly thereafter."

So I drove Alicia up the coast. I cruised around the town while she completed what she had to do and we headed south again. Halfway down, we both decided we needed to eat something. We turned off the thruway. Alicia had heard of an interesting restaurant on the river in Palatka. It overlooked the Saint John River. We parked the car in the lot which fronted directly on the river and went in. We ordered, and I looked over at my companion. It was the first time we'd really been alone together. Here I was, free at last from my fugitive past with the woman I knew I loved to my core being. Could I dare to hope even that it might be reciprocated?

Suddenly, Alicia who was seated across from me facing the dining room jumped perceptively. "Gil, I was lip reading across the room I do it unselfconsciously sometimes and I read 'Hidell!'"

"Don't turn around, I don't think he's seen us, but I'm sure it's him. The moustache is gone and his hair is blonde now, but it's him, I'm sure of it now," her eyes gleamed at me in her excitement. Ah, this was one perfect, beautiful woman, my heart sang. I turned slightly sideways and pretended to peruse a wine list that was sitting upright on the table. It was Hidell. He was with a guy who looked like the classic slacker who hangs around poolrooms and racetracks, a real low life. Probably a minion of Bugloss and Dempster.

The Tally Ho! Was built against the side of a hill. The entrance was actually on the second level above storage rooms which fronted on the river and the parking lot. A balcony ran outside the river view portion of the dining room. It afforded a view of the parking lot and beyond that the river. A boat dock was next door down river and boaters would often patronize The Tally Ho! while on excursions. A ramp with a gravel drive went up from the lot to the main road. A row of highway wooden posts ran along the side of the ramp which fronted towards the river. The posts were strung together by a heavy cable line which ended at the bottom by a triangle formed by a cable guy wire down to the ground of the ramp.

I heard Hidell say to his companion, "Well, Raker, I'll be seeing you Tuesday in Miami," just as Raker was getting up to leave.

"Come on, let's just go out on the balcony, for a minute so Hidell won't see us," I said. Our table was right off the balcony, and the long French doors were open. We both went out as Hidell was leaving cash for the check. We gazed at the river scene. A party from a large boat docked at The Anchory Marina next door was walking across the drive. I sensed that Hidell had left. Then I saw him down below walking to his car. I should have eased Alicia back inside to our table, but something perverse crossed my mind. I suddenly wanted Hidell to see us. I think I wanted to stare him down, to let him know that we'd seen him. There was a little masculine cock-of-the-walk here, too. I wanted to exult in being with Alicia and him seeing me with Alicia. "You got the money, honey, I got the girl" was part of what I was thinking and a bit of "You scum. We're up here staring you down. We know what you did, and we despise you for it." Anyhow, I lingered on the balcony and made no effort to shepherd Alicia back inside. He started the car, it was a Buick—I can still see it, light blue, an old lady's color, I thought, backed it around and started heading toward the up ramp. Suddenly, he looked up right at the two of us. A look of pure horror first, it was totally unexpected to him, then a fraction of a second of uncertainty and unsure if we'd recognized him and the certainty that we had and then panic. It was like a movie in slow motion. Alicia looked like a statue the whole time. A proud victor looking down at her indesert vassal.

He was headed towards the ramp gunning the car, scattering gravel in little clouds, in his haste to escape, but his head seemed glued upward affixed to us and the balcony. He was not paying attention to his driving and misjudged the ramp and the line of heavy guard posts. The car gave a hideous scrunching sound of damaged metal as it literally ran up the low guy cable and sat atop the posts. It perched there with a perfect balance. One post held the car impaled having punctured the passenger side floor board. It teetered. The two guard posts on which the car was resting suddenly flattened from the weight. The car took a sickening slow thwamp into the river and disappeared like a stone. The crowd stood thunderstruck, unable to move. Twenty to thirty patrons of The Tally Ho! had joined us on the balcony drawn by the sounds of Hidell's car attacking the ramp.

I found Alicia in my arms her face buried in my shoulder. "Come on," I whispered to her, "let's get out of here. He's over and done with. There's nothing anyone can do." I led her out to our car. It was an Oldsmobile, of vintage years, which had belonged to Alicia's mother and which stayed at the Palm Beach house permanently to be used when family was in residence. She had started to cry, from shock I think, "Oh it's horrible, horrible," she said over and over.

As we walked to the car it dawned on me that I was walking with her in my arms. Like a "lover" comforting his mate. My God, I think she might love me, could it be she does loves me? It kept rolling around my head together with another recollection not pleasant. The impalement of Hidell's car had the identical look of the fishhook prong in the box that impaled on Sonny's bloody and burning hand. The same hypnotizing horror.

After a few minutes in the car I just held Alicia close and tight until she stopped crying.

I got back out of the car, "let me just take a look to see if they've found the body yet." She nodded without speaking. I walked back to the ramp. The police were there and state troopers. Two volunteers from The Anchory were diving down in the river where the car had disappeared. A crowd of witnesses was standing in a herd off to the side talking to radio and TV crews who were helicoptering in from Jacksonville News. A media circus was in full swing. The divers pulled up the body as I stood there and staggered up the bank to the lot and lay it there on the ground. It was one of those rare moments when everyone involved was preoccupied doing something. The troopers were trying to get a crew together to raise the car, the divers had gone looking for a body bag. The witnesses were schmoozing the film crews trying to get on TV. A blanket had been thrown over the face, but I saw his arm outstretched. A glint shone. I knew instantly that it was the gold ID bracelet. In a trice, (this "trice" I guess from those Basil King novels. Guess I'm getting educated at last) I flicked it from his limp wrist into my pants pocket. Suddenly, the chaos surrounded me again. That one tiny moment of suspended animation was over and not a soul had seen what I'd done. I melted back into the milling throng and returned to the car.

We drove back down the coast in silence. It was the friendly silence of shared experience. Our thoughts had begun working as one entity. We each decided we'd say nothing to Theron. We felt it would needlessly upset him. Hidell was gone, and that was that. I did not experience the exultation of the kill, or the vengeance or the retribution I'd have felt in the past. It was as though that was no longer a part of my character, my psyche.

The next morning by my coffee, Theron had set a local newspaper with a box drawn around a story in the Florida News Section.

Paltaka Police are still trying to piece together the facts involving a fatal accident in the Tally Ho! Restaurant parking lot yesterday afternoon. A car driven by Alexander Hidell apparently jumped a guard—rail at high speed and landed in the St. John River, drowning Mr. Hidell. Police surmise Hidell may have mistaken the gas pedal for the brake. A briefcase found in the car which was hauled from the river late last night indicated he had been comptroller of Salisbury Manufacturing, Inc of Bangor, Maine. This firm recently was purchased by Golconda Holding Co., the huge international defense conglomerate. Police are still looking for next of kin in the Bangor area.

Theron looked at me with a quizzical look. I smiled back all injured innocence. I crooked my finger for him to follow me into the bathroom. He watched as I pulled Hidell's gold bracelet from my pocket, flashed it under his nose to give him a good view, dropped it into the bowl and flushed.

"Let's keep this just between us. No need to upset Alicia." I smiled as we returned to the patio. The cock-of-the-walk had crowed for the last time. The ways of my former life were over.

* * *

Retribution comes in different ways for honorable folk such as the Salisburys. No skullduggery for them. They inherit their retribution. How so? Hidell had no immediate family to inherit his ill-gotten gains. His only heirs at law were Theron Salisbury and Hilda Grindle, our factotum at High Keene. They were both second cousins of the deceased. The two inherited the cash Hidell still had left: $200,000. Hilda had a nest egg to retire on, and Theron gave his share to Alicia. She and I used it to educate our son Kip through Bowdoin and business school. Q.E.D.

My tale is nearing its end. Alicia and I were married by a justice of the peace in the living room of the Palm Beach house. I went to my marriage bed a virgin: "Keep yourself to yourself" to the bitter end! We honeymooned at High Keene. I have no reason to believe Alicia was disappointed in what she found. I spent the first year of our marriage going to business courses learning how to manage money. I guess I learned my lessons there well. A string of nursing homes I amassed over the years was recently sold to a conglomerate for a sum big enough to carry our little family forward for another few generations.

* * *

I look out over the field here at High Keene, the curving gravel drive running out to the road. Ah, there's the flash of the fancy wheel covers on our car turning in from the road. Alicia will be here in a moment. I wonder why I've always bought those titanium spokes and covers for my cars all these years. Silly really. Must be something primal or ancestral . . .

* * *

It was Hilda who found him. She thought he had fallen asleep as she'd looked out the dining room windows periodically to check on him. But then he hadn't moved for awhile, and so she went out on the balcony. Alicia had taken a lengthy phone call right as she'd entered the house from her money manager in New York.

Tears streaming, Hilda ran to her and led her to him. A notebook was opened on his lap and he'd begun to write: "No Alabaster Box" at the top of the page and then the beginning to the opening paragraph: "It was the right time for looking back through time to yesteryear—take stock, look back . . ."

That was all.

Hilda held Alicia and then led her to a chair next to him. Hoping to comfort her, Hilda said, "He was a such a Tom Sawyer-like man, Gil Rushing. Such a wholesome all-American apple pie soul he was. I'm sure he meant to write his memories of a typical American boy, working up through life and all. 'Twould had been such a nice thing for you and Mr. Kip to remember him by." She hugged Alicia tightly. Alicia looked a little puzzled: "I guess you're right" she said. "He said so little about his family. I wonder what that title meant."

Months later, Alicia had gone down to New York. Hilda was cleaning out Gil Rushing's desk at High Keene. She found the little red book. The title sounded vaguely familiar but she couldn't recall where or how. She added it to a pile of stuff going out to Mr. Kip in LA. It would be a nice thing for him to have.

BVG